KISSING MR. KNIGHTLEY

AUSTEN HUNKS
BOOK TWO

VALERIE BOWMAN

JUNE THIRD ENTERPRISES, LLC

She's all about work…

When nurse practitioner Ellie Hoffman agrees to help her best friend's newly rich and famous country music star brother, she's not worried about falling for his legendary charm. Ellie's known Luke Knightley since childhood, and she's well aware of his reputation as a smooth-talking player. She's not about to fall for his tricks—after all, she's a certified player-hater through and through.

He's all about play…

Luke may have it all—a sprawling mansion in Nashville, a private jet, a chart-topping album—but a recent betrayal has left him questioning who he can trust. When a tour bus accident leaves him in need of some serious TLC, Ellie, his childhood friend and eternal critic, is the first person he turns to.

Can they find common ground…with a kiss?

But as Ellie tends to Luke's wounds, sparks fly in unexpected ways. Can they keep their relationship strictly professional when kisses start to redefine the job description?

CHAPTER 1

A Friday in June — Ellie

"Oh, absolutely not." The words slipped out before I could stop them—sharp, final.

"You're not even going to hear me out?" Meg asked, eyebrows raised across the table.

We were having lunch at our favorite noodle shop near the campus of Everton College in Milwaukee, where Meg was a history professor and my closest friend.

I leaned back in my chair, arms crossed. "There's nothing to hear. I'm not flying across the country to babysit your rockstar brother."

Meg gave me a look– the one that said *you're being impossible.* And okay, maybe I was. But this was *Luke Knightley* we were talking about. Walking ego with a guitar. Nashville's newest country prince. And—unfortunately—my childhood nemesis. Or, at least, that's how I've always chosen to see him. The man had left a trail of broken hearts wider than I-94 and teased me mercilessly every time I was in the same zip code.

"Look," I added, softening—slightly—"I'm sorry he got hurt. I really am. That tour bus crash could've been so much worse."

Meg nodded. "I know. I was scared out of my mind when I got the call."

That tugged at something inside me. A quiet flicker of guilt. I'd seen Meg cry exactly twice in our nearly lifelong friendship. Once over her grandmother. The other when she got tenure. If she was asking me for a favor, she had to mean it.

Still...

"I became a nurse to help people," I said, nudging my noodles around the bowl. "People who need me. Not people who I've been sparring with since puberty."

Meg sighed. "A patient is a patient."

"I treat strangers. Not...Luke." My voice had that too-sharp edge again. Ugh. I knew I sounded petty, but when it came to her brother, maturity wasn't my strong suit.

Meg sighed and leaned in. "He doesn't trust anyone right now. The last nurse sold pictures of him to a gossip site."

My stomach turned. "That's...awful."

"One of the photos was of him *sleeping*, Ellie. Can you imagine how violated he must've felt?"

Okay, that was worse than awful. "And the nurse was fired, right? Maybe even sued?"

"Of course. But now the insurance company insists on a full-time home health provider while his arm heals. They say he's a liability without one—especially since his hands are..."

"His moneymakers. Got it." I stabbed a piece of bok choy with unnecessary force. "There are thousands of nurses out there. Some of them would probably fight to rub ointment on Luke Knightley's abs."

She ignored that. "Luke asked for someone he knows. Someone he trusts."

That gave me pause. Luke trusted me? That was news. Any time we'd been in the same room together in the last ten years, we'd done nothing but trade insults. And not even thinly veiled ones.

"I didn't even know he liked me," I muttered. "He's spent most of his life calling me 'Nurse Ratched,' as you may recall."

"He teases people he likes," Meg said, shrugging as if all the times Luke and I had been at each other's throats were no big deal. "And you call him Rockabilly, so I figure you're even."

"Yeah, well, we're not in second grade anymore," I replied automatically, though the words rang hollow.

Because once—just once—he'd teased me in a way that felt dangerously close to wanting more. And I hadn't forgotten how quickly that moment passed.

Meg gave me the puppy-dog eyes. They only ever worked on me with Mindy, my favorite oncology patient back at Milwaukee Children's—who also knew how to manipulate me into sneaking in contraband candy.

"Don't look at me like that," I grumbled.

"You could help him. For real."

"I'm a nurse practitioner," I countered. "I'm expensive."

"Luke is rich now," she said with a shrug. "He could afford to pay you double your rate."

I hesitated. Damn it.

Double my rate would help with my student loans. Maybe even let me take a break from the hospital. Hadn't my boss, Lena, been nagging me for months to take an extended vacation?

But I didn't take vacations. I didn't even take long lunches.

And this wasn't exactly a break—I'd be taking care of someone. Again.

I shook my head. "It's not just the money. It's…everything. The past. The way he treats me."

Meg nodded. "What if I make him promise to be sweet and respectful?"

I snorted. "Sweet Luke Knightley? That's an oxymoron."

"He's changed. He really has."

I studied her face. There was no sign of sarcasm. Just concern. And maybe hope.

She grabbed the check before I could. "Just say you'll think about it."

I let out a long breath, stood, and slung my bag over my shoulder. "Fine. I'll think about it."

Which, translated from Ellie-speak, meant *absolutely not*. But if it got Meg off my back…

Still, as I walked out into the Milwaukee summer sunshine, I felt a flicker of something I couldn't quite name. Was it curiosity? Nostalgia? Regret?

I shook it off.

No. I'm *not* working for Luke Knightley.

But I couldn't help but wonder if I meant it. Or if I just needed to convince myself I did.

CHAPTER 2

Friday afternoon — Ellie

Doing rounds on the children's ward always made me feel better. I loved this place so much that I'd volunteered to be the chair of the annual fundraising gala.

As I stepped out of the elevator onto the Oncology Ward, the words I'd told Meg earlier echoed in my head. I *had* become a nurse to help people.

Like Mindy.

The fluorescent lights buzzed overhead, the usual chorus of beeping monitors and hallway chatter humming in the background. Mindy's room was at the end of the hall, and even before I reached it, I could hear the sound of Taylor Swift blaring through the cracked door.

I knocked twice, then pushed it open. "Tay-Tay at top volume," I said. "Nice."

Mindy grinned from her pillow, bright pink scarf wrapped around her bald head like a fashion statement. "It's for healing. Obviously."

"Ah, yes. The Swift Method. Very cutting edge."

She pointed at me dramatically. "You joke, but this playlist is scientifically proven to lower stress and increase fabulousness."

"Well then," I said, moving to check her IV, "let me get out of the way of the miracle cure."

Mindy was fourteen, wildly opinionated, and halfway through chemo. She was also one of my favorites—though we weren't supposed to say that.

I'd first met her six months ago. Since then, I'd become her snack mule, playlist manager, and the sole adult she allowed to do her dressing changes without making a scene.

Today, she narrowed her eyes at me.

"You're thinking about something," she said.

"I'm always thinking about something."

"Nope. You've got your 'should I or shouldn't I' face."

I gave her a look. "I do not have that face."

"You totally do. Spill."

I hesitated. "My friend Meg wants me to take a short-term private job."

"Here? Or somewhere fun?"

"Nashville."

Mindy gasped like I'd just announced a trip to the moon. "Music City? Oh my God, Ellie, do it! Who is it? Is it someone famous?"

I sighed. "Yes. Unfortunately."

"A guy?" Her eyebrows inched up.

"Maybe."

"A hot guy?" Now they were at full mast.

"No more questions."

"Who?" She practically leaped off the bed.

"Pretty sure I shouldn't tell you that. Confidential."

She flailed. "Ellie, you can't just *not* go be the personal nurse to a hot, wounded celebrity. This is like…my dream fanfic."

"I'm not going to Nashville to live your fanfic."

"You could be his nurse *and* fall in love. It's the perfect meet-cute."

"We already met," I said. "We grew up together. Pretty sure he once put gum in my hair."

"Even better! That's enemies-to-lovers. Classic arc."

I snorted. "You've been on Wattpad again, haven't you?"

Mindy just grinned and raised a brow. "Go. Live a little."

I smiled back, but deep down, the truth curled tight in my chest…

I wasn't afraid of going—I was afraid of what might happen if I stayed.

CHAPTER 3

Saturday morning — Luke

"What did she say?" I asked the moment Meg answered my call.

"Umm. She's thinking about it."

Meg might've held a Ph.D. in early nineteenth-century British history, but subtlety was not my sister's superpower. Her voice always pitched up like she was hiding a body.

"She said no, didn't she?" I groaned.

"At first," Meg admitted.

"And you talked her into it?" I was doubtful. It would take more than Meg's questionable charm to convince Elenor Hoffman to drop everything and come to Nashville to nurse me back to health.

Ellie hated me. Or she pretended to. That was our thing. We bickered constantly but always rallied for Meg—our shared person, our reason for tolerating each other.

Ellie had been in my orbit since we were kids. She was Meg's best friend. Always around. Always giving me grief.

Somewhere around high school, when I was a junior and she was a freshman, we started trading barbs like it was a competitive sport. I couldn't even remember how it started—it just became our rhythm. And weirdly? I liked it. Our strange, combative non-friendship was the longest relationship I'd ever had with a woman I wasn't related to. Probably because we'd never tried to date. Not seriously, anyway.

There was one time. Just one.

Nothing really happened, but sometimes I wondered what it would have been like if it had.

Not that it mattered now.

And me? I don't do commitment. I'm wildly allergic to it. Short-term, no strings, just fun—that's my jam.

Ellie, on the other hand, thought I was a train wreck. Which… Okay, maybe she wasn't completely wrong. Especially back when I was crashing on Meg's couch and hustling gigs with my band around Milwaukee. Meanwhile, Ellie was all grown-up and stable—certified nurse practitioner, solid job, and the type of adult who probably meal prepped.

I thought she was uptight. Super hot, granted. But a real control freak. And yeah, I gave her hell for it. Constantly.

Now, karma had circled back. Because I needed her.

And that wasn't a position I was used to being in. In fact, I prided myself on being pretty damn self-sufficient.

After graduating from Stanford, I'd stuck around California, worked as a structural engineer, and hated it. Hated it enough that on my thirtieth birthday, I quit. Packed it all in and went back to Milwaukee to chase music full-time.

Three years later, it paid off. My band finally hit. We got signed, moved to Nashville, and life looked like a dream.

Until the tour bus crash.

Three weeks ago, coming around some godforsaken mountain curve in North Carolina, our bus flipped. A window shattered, a metal shard nailed me in the shoulder, and I broke my left arm. No guitar. No touring. No choice but to press pause on my whole life.

The label, the tour company, and the insurance folks all agreed: postpone the tour until fall so I could heal properly.

It sucked. But it got worse.

Because some home health nurse hired by the insurance company decided to sneak photos of me—yes, including one where my junk made a surprise appearance on the internet.

That image was now somewhere in a tabloid archive, probably next to a blurry Bigfoot photo.

She got fired, obviously. But the damage was done.

No more strangers in my house. Period.

I'd been doing fine on my own. The weekly house-call doc said my arm and shoulder were healing well. But the label insisted on a full-time nurse. Their hands were tied by the insurance company's requirements.

So I needed someone I could trust.

Unfortunately, that list had exactly one name on it.

Nurse Ratched.

Ellie hated that nickname, which made it even more satisfying to use. But now, all that teasing might have blown up in my face.

Meg had tried, clearly. But if Ellie wasn't convinced yet, it was time I stepped in. Groveling wasn't my strong suit, but I was officially desperate.

"Give me her number," I said.

"She didn't say I could," Meg replied.

I closed my eyes, exhaling slowly. "I'm not going to show up at her door with a boombox, Meg."

"Still. Three-way call or nothing."

"Fine." Probably for the best. If Ellie saw my name on the screen, she might ignore it—or worse, block me mid-ring.

I cleared my throat, preparing myself for verbal combat.

Then I sent up a silent prayer to the deity of hot, tightly wound nurse practitioners.

Let the groveling begin.

CHAPTER 4

Two seconds later — Ellie

My phone lit up, and the *Gilmore Girls* theme spilled from the speaker.

Meg. Of course.

We'd watched the show religiously growing up, the two of us curled on the couch with popcorn and way too much emotion for our age. Now the ringtone was a warning bell.

I already knew what this call was about.

Luke.

I debated letting it go to voicemail. But in the end, I swiped to answer.

"Hello?"

"Good morning, Ellie."

Oh, wow. Meg sounded way too enthusiastic. "I know why you're calling," I said flatly. "And the answer is—"

"Luke's on the line. He wants to talk to you." Her voice dropped to a rushed whisper, like she was handing off a grenade.

Seriously?

"Meg—" I started, teeth clenched.

Too late.

"Hi, Ellie. It's Luke."

His voice came through low and rough—of course it did. Damn professional musicians and their unfair vocal cords.

My pulse stuttered anyway. Because that voice still hit in places I didn't want to examine.

I sat back against the pillows, determined to stay composed. I wasn't eighteen anymore. I wasn't even twenty-eight. I was thirty-two, highly educated, and had a job that regularly demanded I explain complex treatment plans to surgeons who didn't like being questioned. I could handle a phone call with Luke Knightley.

"Hey, Luke," I said, keeping my voice even. Calm. Professional.

"I need a favor," he said. "A big one. And before I ask—I know I've been a jackass. I've said things I shouldn't have. But I need your help, Ellie. I wouldn't be asking if I wasn't desperate."

Well. That wasn't what I'd expected.

Normally, Luke greeted me with sarcasm. A nickname I hated. A smirk I could hear through the phone. But today? He sounded…vulnerable. And sincere.

I wasn't sure I liked it. It threw me off-balance.

"A lot's changed for you, huh?" I said. My tone stayed casual, but I was already slipping into medical professional mode—calm, measured, in control. Small talk was my armor. Easier than reacting to how raw he sounded.

"Yeah," he said, sighing. "Some good changes. Some not so great."

I wanted him to say something cocky, something dismissive, so I could find my righteous anger again. But he wasn't making it easy.

"Meg told me you weren't interested," he continued. "But

I was hoping you might come down. Just talk to me. In person."

I blinked. "You want me to come to Nashville?"

"I'll cover everything—flight, food, whatever you need. No pressure. Just hear me out. And if you still want to say no afterward, I'll respect that."

Damn him. He sounded like a functioning adult. Even more surprising, he sounded genuine. Calm. Respectful, even. None of the usual baiting or games.

He'd even called me Ellie.

Meg had mentioned how nice his house was, and—fine— I'd seen it in a celebrity real estate roundup online. It was ridiculous. Elegant. Understated. Nothing like the kid I remembered growing up next to in the trailer park.

I shouldn't have been curious. But part of me wanted to see what success looked like on someone who used to tease me about my pigtails.

I also wanted to know if the man I'd quietly crushed on since high school had become someone I still recognized.

The idea of being flown out, no strings attached, was hard to pass up. Lena would be thrilled if I took a couple of days off, and I'd be back in plenty of time for my weekly visit with Mindy next Friday.

It wasn't lost on me that Luke had somehow turned this into an offer I'd be ridiculous to refuse.

"Okay," I heard myself say. "I'll come down. But that's it. No promises."

"That's all I'm asking."

His voice softened—grateful, maybe even relieved. And that…was a problem.

Because a grateful Luke Knightley was a little bit hard to resist.

CHAPTER 5

An hour later — Ellie

The call connected on the second ring.

"Ellie-bean!" Grandma's voice crackled through the landline like it had something to prove. She refused to use the cellphone I bought her for anything but emergencies, and even then, it usually lived under a pile of mail and three half-finished crossword puzzles.

"Hi, Gran." I sank onto the edge of my bed, curling my legs underneath me. The hum of my air purifier filled the silence. "How are you feeling today?"

"Oh, you know. Woke up breathing. That's a win."

I smiled. "Did you take your meds?"

"I took my meds, ate my toast, and yelled at *Wheel of Fortune* like it owes me rent. I'm thriving."

"Sounds like you've got it covered."

"If I really had it covered, I'd be in a hot tub with Sam Elliott and a bottle of tequila. But what are you gonna do?"

I chuckled. "Everything in moderation, Gran."

"That's what I told the nurse at the clinic. She said I only get one vice, so I picked sarcasm."

There was a pause. Then, "You sound tired, bean."

I flopped back on my pillows. "I am. Work's been nonstop. Long hours, emotional stuff. And then there's this… situation."

"A man?" she said instantly, like she'd been waiting all day for the gossip.

"Gran."

"What? I'm old, not dead. Spill it. Is he cute? Employed? Capable of holding a conversation without quoting Joe Rogan?"

I laughed, then sighed. "It's not like that. He's a friend—kind of. Luke Knightley. He's injured. Meg wants me to be his live-in nurse for a few weeks while he recovers."

Gran knew Meg and Luke. She'd watched them grow up right alongside me.

Gran was quiet for a beat. "And?"

"And I'm considering it."

"Well. I'm the last person to discourage an adventure. Especially when a good-looking man is involved. Does Luke still have the hair and the dimples?"

"Yep," I replied, popping the *p*. "As far as I know."

"Then what are you waiting for?"

"You're incorrigible, you know that?"

"If that's a twenty-cent word for feisty, I'll take it."

I shook my head. "It's not that simple, Gran." I sighed. "The kids need me, and the gala's coming up, and—"

"Sounds like a lot of excuses if you ask me."

"Are you actually encouraging me to go spend time with an emotionally unavailable man?"

"Oh, honey." Her voice softened. "You are the most responsible person I know—and I mean that as a compliment. You've been running on fumes for months. You're always the one holding everything together. You can't forget to hold on to yourself too."

That landed hard.

Gran had practically raised me. My mom had me at seventeen and treated motherhood like a part-time gig she didn't want. She took off when I was six and resurfaced every couple of years with a new boyfriend and a fresh excuse. My dad? He existed, allegedly. But I couldn't have picked him out of a lineup.

Gran was the one who packed my lunches, taught me to drive, and cheered at my nursing school graduation like the whole thing had been thrown just for me. I paid her bills now—electric, internet, and the cable package with the obscure murder channels she loved. It was the least I could do.

She was my only real family. The only one who'd ever stayed.

So yeah, I didn't need a therapist to explain my attraction to unavailable men. That was straight out of the Daddy Issues Playbook. Chapter One: Fall for the guy who's going to leave. Illustration: Luke Knightley.

"I don't want to leave you either, Gran," I added quietly.

"Oh, please. I've got Phyllis from the center, Rosie next door, and a fridge full of bougie soups from that fancy meal delivery service you bought me. I'll survive."

I laughed. "Well, Luke asked me to come check it out. Just to see."

"Then go."

"But it's *Luke*, Gran. And…"

"And he's a heartbreaker. Always was. But you're not made of glass, sweetheart. And the handsome ones?" Her voice dipped conspiratorially. "They're usually good for a story. Or at least a few unforgettable kisses."

"Gran!"

She chuckled. "I'm just saying. Nobody writes a novel about the girl who stayed home and alphabetized the vitamin drawer. Go see what happens."

CHAPTER 6

Two hours later — Luke

The house was too damn quiet.

No whirring coffee grinder. No studio hum. No guitar pick slapping strings in rhythm. Just the occasional creak of floorboards and Dolly's claws tapping across them like she was pacing out my existential crisis.

She was a Brittany spaniel—sweet, spoiled, overly empathetic—and clearly concerned that her human had turned into a useless lump with a hurt shoulder and no snacks to share. She trotted into the room, tail wagging halfheartedly, then flopped onto her bed with a sigh loud enough to rival mine.

I sat on the edge of the couch, guitar in my lap like a prosthetic I hadn't figured out how to use yet. My fingers hovered near the frets. Right hand: functional. Left arm: dead weight.

I strummed.

The sound came out broken—ragged and uneven, like the guitar itself had given up on me.

Dolly whined softly from across the room.

"You and me both," I muttered.

I leaned back and stared at the ceiling. Three weeks since the accident. Three weeks of missed interviews, scrapped studio time, and charity appearances passed off to someone who could smile without wincing.

But that wasn't the hardest part. The hardest part was how unsafe I felt—everywhere, even at home. The crash had shaken my body, but the betrayal afterward? That cracked something deeper. I was unraveling in ways I didn't know how to stop.

For the first time in my life, I was seeing a therapist.

A quiet knock on the doorframe broke the spiral.

Remington leaned in, holding a green smoothie that looked like regret in a plastic bottle.

Jeremy had been my best friend since high school. Woodworker. Walking lumberjack. Meg's boyfriend. Currently living in my guest wing while he built custom cabinetry, bookshelves, and—last I checked—an entire walk-in closet out of reclaimed barn wood because, of course, I hired my best friend the second I got rich.

"You look like hell," he said cheerfully.

"Thanks," I said. "That's what I was going for."

He tossed me the smoothie. I missed it, obviously. It landed with a soft thud on the pillow beside me. Dolly didn't even flinch.

"You're not gonna drink that, are you?" he said in an accusatory tone.

I eyed it. "Does it taste like blended grass and guilt?"

"Of course."

"Then no."

Remington didn't sit—he just leaned against the doorframe like he always did, casual but observant. The kind of guy who noticed when your mood changed even if your words didn't.

After a beat, he said, "Meg told me Ellie's coming with her down here tomorrow."

I didn't look at him. "Yeah."

"You sure this is a good idea?"

"Nope."

"But you asked her anyway."

I pinned the bottle between my knees and twisted off the lid one-handed. Took a sip. Kale—of course. Bleck. "It's only temporary."

"Is it?"

I looked at him.

Remington shrugged. "Just saying. You've been weird about Ellie for years. What happens when she shows up here, all competent and nurturing and…?"

"Hot?" I supplied.

Remington shook his head. "I wasn't gonna say that."

"Good." My jaw tightened. "Anyway, it's not like that."

He grinned. "It's *exactly* like that."

I didn't answer. Just stared out the window at the sprawling backyard. Birds chirped like they didn't know the world had gone off script.

"I almost kissed her once," I said.

Remington's brows lifted. "You? The king of casual? Almost kissed your sister's best friend? That's basically a marriage proposal."

I scrunched up my nose. "One night, after a party at Meg's place—years ago now—we were both in the kitchen, everyone else had either left or passed out. Ellie was wearing this ratty nursing school sweatshirt and drinking red wine that made her lips pink."

Remington raised an eyebrow.

"I almost kissed her," I repeated. "I wanted to. She looked at me like she was waiting for it."

"But you didn't?"

"Nope."

"Why not?"

"Because I was me. And she was…Ellie. Smart, stable, way too good for drunk, aimless me." I shrugged with my uninjured shoulder. "I made a joke instead. And then it was over."

Remington scratched his beard, thoughtful. "And now she's going to be living in your house. Taking care of you. Hands-on."

"Yeah."

"And you're still…interested?"

I gave him a look. "I haven't *not* thought about that night in years."

Remington nodded again, quiet. Then, "You sure it's a good idea if she's your nurse, then?"

I sighed. "No. Not even a little."

He smiled. "But you're doing it anyway?"

"Absolutely."

He pushed off the doorframe. "Then try not to screw it up."

I smirked. "You saying that as my friend, or as Meg's boyfriend?"

He walked away, calling over his shoulder, "Both."

Dolly snorted from her bed like she agreed.

I expelled my breath in a rush. Tomorrow, Ellie would walk through that door. And I'd have to figure out how to look her in the eye when part of me still wanted to rewind time and fix what I never had the courage to start.

Sunday — Ellie

"I knew he was rich," I muttered, eyeing the champagne on ice and the buttery leather seats as we boarded the private jet the next day. "But this is rich-rich."

Meg grinned as she followed me up the steps. "Luke's house has two pools. Indoor and outdoor."

"I saw," I muttered, choosing not to mention my internet deep dive to Meg. Even thought it was purely professional. Curiosity was a natural part of nursing, wasn't it?

"He doesn't own the jet though," Meg added. "He rents it. I think."

"Oh, poor guy," I deadpanned.

We settled into the kind of seats you wanted to rub your face on, and a flight attendant materialized with champagne flutes already filled. She handed them over with a perfect smile.

"Mr. Knightley welcomes you both and looks forward to your visit in Nashville," she said.

I choked on a laugh. "Mr. Knightley? What is this, a

Regency reboot?" I glanced at Meg. "I'm never calling him that."

"Good," she mouthed.

The flight was quick—like, time-warp quick—and I spent most of it peppering Meg with questions about Luke's injuries and trying very hard not to ask how many groupies hung out at his house.

"One whiff of sarcasm and I'm gone," I said for the fifth time. "I'll rent a car, buy a bike, ride a goat, whatever it takes to get back to Milwaukee."

"He knows," Meg said, unbothered, sipping her champagne like she was already on vacation.

We landed at a small airstrip where a black Range Rover waited on the tarmac. The driver wore a suit, gloves, and an expressionless face. "Mr. Knightley welcomes you to Nashville," he said. "May I assist you into the vehicle?"

Everything was smooth. Polished. Precise. Like Luke had a personal concierge team choreographing our arrival.

"Rich-people travel is superior," I whispered to Meg as we drove toward Belle Meade.

Luke's neighborhood looked like Pinterest had merged with a luxury real estate site. When we finally pulled into his tree-lined drive, I spotted the white-brick mansion and actual copper-roofed cupolas. As we stepped out, a security team quietly sprang into motion—gloved hands on luggage, earpieces buzzing, gatehouse surveillance tracking our movements.

"Are we in *Succession*?" I muttered.

"You're not wrong," Meg replied.

The gate opened after some invisible signal. "This way, Ms. Hoffman, Ms. Knightley," one of the guards said.

"How do they all know our names?" I whispered.

"Luke probably emailed a dossier," Meg whispered back.

As we passed a courtyard fountain with an open book sculpture, I paused. "Really? A book?"

"What? Luke loves to read," Meg said.

"Sure. If beer labels count."

She shook her head.

Inside, the mudroom looked like a magazine spread. Built-in cabinets, patterned cushions, monogrammed leashes, and two pristine dog beds. "Jeremy's work?" I asked, running a hand over the glossy wood.

"Yep."

We moved through a corridor and into a kitchen so beautiful I nearly forgot to breathe. Seafoam-blue cabinetry, twin quartz islands, Viking appliances, and actual fresh white roses in crystal vases. It smelled like rosemary, money, and unattainable dreams.

"This is where he makes toast?" I asked.

"He has a chef. Her name is Linda."

"Of course he does."

The kitchen led into a "sitting room"—which was larger than most Milwaukee apartments—with chocolate-brown velvet couches and mood lighting. The security guard gestured. "Please wait here. Mr. Knightley will be down shortly."

"Thanks," I said, sinking into the couch.

Meg leaned over and whispered, "Custom. A hundred grand. Each."

I shot back to my feet like the cushions were lava. "A hundred thousand? Per couch?"

Before I could spiral further, Luke strolled in.

He was wearing forest-green flannel with dark jeans and no shoes. His dark hair was tousled like he'd just rolled out of bed looking infuriatingly hot and, as usual, his blue eyes sparkled with mischief.

"Meg!" he said, greeting his sister with a half-hug that avoided the dark sling on his left arm.

I stayed back, watching the golden boy of Twin Valley Mobile Home Park walk through his castle like it was no big deal. He looked…annoyingly amazing. Which made sense. Luke had always been good-looking. Even in middle school, when the rest of us were awkward, he had that smug, magnetic thing going on. Now he was all grown up and the smug had turned devastating.

He turned to me. "Hi, Ellie."

"Rockabilly," I said coolly, like I hadn't just imagined him shirtless two seconds ago.

His smile was blinding. "How was your flight?"

"Quick."

"And the car?"

"Very plush." My voice was steady. I was proud.

"You look amazing," he said.

Damn him. "Thanks. You too." I said it because I'm polite, not because he looked like a country-music catalog model.

"I hope you like the guest room I picked out for you," he added.

"She should see the whole house," Meg piped up.

I shot her a look. She ignored me.

Luke nodded. "I'll have Mrs. Hawthorne show you up. I'll meet you there in thirty?"

My eyes narrowed. "Mrs. Hawthorne?"

"My housekeeper."

Naturally.

Meg gave me a quick wave and vanished, clearly headed to find Jeremy, who was obviously somewhere building more custom cabinetry for his rich best friend.

As I turned to follow Mrs. Hawthorne, who had materialized from the fancy shadows, I looked back. Luke stood at the base of the staircase, smiling faintly, watching me climb.

"I'll see you at 2:30, Ellie," he said, voice smooth and low.

The way he said my name sent a shiver down my spine.

I reminded myself—again—that this was a job. A favor. Not the start of anything. And not even a job...yet. Only a look and see.

And yet...as I followed the housekeeper into the next chapter of this ridiculous fairy tale, I wasn't so sure.

CHAPTER 8

Half an hour later — Luke

One thing I'd always known about Ellie Hoffman: she didn't just dislike lateness—she treated it like a crime. When we were kids, she once locked me out of Meg's birthday party because I was ten minutes late.

As a nurse practitioner now, being on time wasn't just a habit, it was how she functioned—precise, punctual, sharp as hell. Me? I figured give or take thirty minutes was close enough. She'd roasted me for it more than once. But now that I was trying to convince her to be my nurse, I'd actually set an alarm to make sure I wasn't late. Growth.

I'd given her the best guest room—vaulted ceilings, garden views, and a tub you could swim laps in. I even kicked Remington out for it. He didn't say a word about how long I stared at the linen closet debating between two damn guest robes.

I knocked on the big white door that led to her room. When the door opened, my brain stalled. Ellie stood there in black leggings and a fitted sweater, her blonde hair down in soft waves, and for one second, I forgot how to form words.

I managed a sound. Something between a cough and a whimper. Real smooth.

She'd always been beautiful. That wasn't new. But now it hit differently. Maybe because she wasn't just Meg's best friend anymore—she was *here*, in my house, staying in my guest room, wearing my favorite kind of sweater.

Off-limits had never felt quite so tempting.

I lifted my hand to my head, the move automatic. Nervous tell. Not exactly my usual vibe. But Ellie wasn't just another pretty face. And this wasn't just another night.

I'd screwed up a lot of relationships. I was always the variable that didn't solve. But this time, I couldn't afford to get the math wrong.

But standing there, staring at Ellie, all I could think about was how hard my cock was and how intensely inappropriate *that* was. I was trying to hire this woman to help me. I had no intention of sexually harassing her while I was at it. Was getting a hard-on considered sexual harassment? Probably. Damn it. I had no control over it. I merely hoped she wouldn't notice.

"Hi," I said stupidly, still pressing my hand to the top of my head.

"Hi," she replied, and the bright smile she gave me did nothing to stop the rising appreciation in my jeans.

"How do you like your room?" I asked.

Being nice to Ellie was weird. My instincts wanted to call her Nurse Ratched or ask if the bug up her ass had settled in for the winter. But I couldn't—

A. I needed her help.
B. I'd promised Meg I'd be nice.

Well, *sweet*, technically, but that felt like trying to put a sundress on a bear. This? This was me trying.

Ellie turned to glance around, giving me the moment I needed to step inside and discreetly adjust the situation in my pants.

"It's absolutely gorgeous," she said. "Especially the flowers."

"Yeah." I crossed to the table where the bouquet sat. "All the high-end hotels do it. My decorator insisted."

"Your decorator has excellent taste."

Relief, unexpected and sharp, moved through me. I always worried the place looked like I was trying too hard. Ellie knew where I came from—sheet-for-a-bedroom-door days. If she approved, maybe I was doing something right.

"You're not just saying that because I'm your patient, are you?" I asked.

She smirked. "If I was being nice out of pity, you'd have to be on your deathbed."

I exhaled. "Thank God. I've been dying to call you Nurse Ratched since you got here."

"Careful," she warned, dragging her tongue slowly across her bottom lip, sending another bolt of heat through me. "I didn't say I'd let you be an ass. But I think some well-timed name-calling might keep things from getting weird."

"Agreed. And for the record, I wasn't mean to you."

She raised a brow so high it could've knocked satellites out of orbit.

"Okay, maybe a little. Occasionally. But I've matured, Nurse Jackie. I'm reformed."

"That remains to be seen," she said, shaking her head, her hair cascading over her shoulders like she was temptation incarnate.

I resisted the urge to reach out and touch it. Barely.

"Wanna see the rest of the house?" I asked, desperate for a

distraction. Anything to stop thinking about her hair. What the hell was wrong with me anyway? When had I ever thought about Ellie's hair? I mean, it had been a hot minute since I'd gotten laid. A broken arm and trust issues will do that to a guy. But the lusting over Ellie had to stop.

"I'd love to," she shot back.

We took the back staircase down to the basement, her shoulder brushing mine on the way. I opened the door to the first room. "This is the gym."

Ellie's brows rose. "Impressive. I never pegged you as a treadmill kind of guy."

"I'm not. My manager is. Something about maintaining the brand." I gestured to the weights. "Turns out being on camera isn't great for the ego."

"Is working out actually in your contract?" she asked, her tone half teasing, half serious.

"No, but I think they tried. There was definitely a clause about 'maintaining aesthetic expectations.'"

She laughed and wandered to the yoga mats in front of the wall-length mirror. "You own yoga mats?"

"They came with the gym package," I admitted. "But don't act surprised. I'm very bendy."

Ellie rolled her eyes but smiled. That smile did more damage to my insides than a set of crunches.

I moved us along to the next room. "Post-workout recovery. Sauna, hot tub, steam room, cold plunge."

She opened the sauna door. A puff of eucalyptus-scented steam rolled out. "You're telling me you actually use this stuff?"

"I mean…the hot tub, yeah. The cold plunge is for people who hate themselves."

She laughed again, and it hit me in the chest. "You have a nice laugh," I said before I could stop myself.

She looked surprised. "You never said that before."

"Never heard it enough."

Ellie's smile faltered for a beat. Something passed between us—quiet, real—before she looked away and pointed to the next room.

The game room. Safer ground.

"Pool table, poker, pinball, electric darts," I listed, giving her space to shake it off.

"You've thought of everything," she said, trailing a finger over the foosball table. "Do you even play half of this?"

"Sometimes. Mostly when I'm avoiding writing songs or dealing with life."

She cocked her head at me. "Relatable."

We paused by the bar. "Beer on tap," she noted.

"Milwaukee pride," I said. "But I've got wine upstairs."

"Don't tell me you drink wine now."

"Nope. But I have it for when wine snobs like you visit." I winked at her.

She smiled again—a real one this time—and it felt like I'd won something I didn't know I was playing for.

After quickly showing her the indoor pool, I led her into the recording studio next, flipping on the lights.

Her eyes went wide. "This is incredible."

"The walls are soundproofed. Remington did them." I motioned toward the gear. "Mic, guitars, sound booth. This is my space."

She walked slowly to the wall, trailing her hand over the wood panels. "It's beautiful." She took a beat. "It feels like… you."

Something about the way she said it made me pause.

"No one's ever said that before," I told her.

Ellie glanced over her shoulder. "Seriously?"

"Seriously." I motioned for her to sit on the loveseat while I lowered myself into the nearby chair. "Most people walk in here, make a joke about me living out my rock star fantasy, and then ask if I can get them concert tickets."

She wrinkled her nose. "That's bleak."

"Yeah." I ran my hand over the worn leather armrest. "But this room's the one place that still feels normal. No press. No expectations. Just sound."

Ellie leaned back into the cushions, looking around with a quiet sort of awe. "How long did it take to build all this?"

"Four months. Give or take. Remington says it's his proudest project, which is big talk coming from a guy who once built a spiral staircase without using a single nail."

She smiled, but her attention was now focused on the sleek microphone setup behind the glass of the recording booth.

"Do you miss it?" she asked. "Being on tour?"

I nodded. "More than I expected to. But mostly I feel bad about letting everyone down. The music isn't just mine anymore."

Ellie turned toward me, brows knitting. "What do you mean?"

I paused, searching for the right words. "Back when we were crashing on floors and playing tiny clubs, music felt… self-indulgent. Like some reckless dream I was chasing just for me. But now? People write to say my songs helped them get through something—heartbreak, grief, whatever. That kind of thing—it changes how you write, how you show up."

She went quiet for a second, then said, "That 'Summer Nights' song? The one with the slow build and the bridge that makes everyone cry?"

I gave a sheepish shrug. "Yeah?"

"That song made me feel less alone when my patient, Mindy, was in the ICU."

My chest tightened. "I didn't know that."

"Well, I didn't exactly send fan mail."

"Still," I said. "That means a lot."

She glanced toward the piano keyboard. "Do you still write? Even with the injury?"

"I try," I admitted. "Mostly lyrics. I jot things down in my phone or hum voice memos. I can't really play the guitar…or the piano since the accident."

Ellie glanced at the sling over my arm. "Must be hard. Not being able to play."

"It sucks," I admitted. "Especially since I'm left-handed."

She winced. "Oof. That's brutal."

"Let's go," I said. Standing, I led her out before I said something vulnerable or stupid.

Next up: the theater. I opened the door with a flourish.

"Popcorn not included," I said.

Ellie stepped inside, eyes widening at the recliners, the massive screen. "You don't do anything halfway, do you?"

"Nope. All the fun of going to the movies, none of the threat of being mobbed."

Her expression shifted—like she suddenly remembered that was my life now. She didn't say anything, and I appreciated the hell out of that.

We climbed the stairs back to the kitchen and ended up in the foyer.

"I swear this space is bigger than my first apartment," she said, turning in a slow circle to stare up at the giant golden chandelier.

"No more curtain doors for me."

I flipped the chandelier switch, lowering the fixture. Her mouth fell open.

"Is this a joke?"

"Apparently it's for cleaning," I muttered.

She touched my arm. Not dramatically—just a hand on skin—but it felt like someone dropped a live wire on me.

"Luke, this is amazing. Really. This entire house. You should be proud."

The lump in my throat showed up uninvited. I swallowed hard.

"Yeah. Thanks."

Only three women in my world had ever seen what I came from—Meg, Mom, and Ellie. Only Ellie had said something like that without obligation. It landed. Hard.

I steered us into the formal rooms, which I never used, then into the music room, where my grand piano sat gleaming under the light.

"You still play?" she asked, trailing a hand across the keys.

"When I can." I glanced at the sling.

She smiled at me again and then followed me across the hall to the library. The room was filled with bookshelves from floor to ceiling.

When I opened the door, she gasped. "What is *this*?"

"My nerd room," I said. "Welcome to it."

She stepped over to the nearest shelf and ran her fingers over the spines. "*War and Peace? Anna Karenina?*"

"Favorites."

Her brow arched. Skepticism practically dripped from her face. "*You've* read these?"

I put my hand on my hip. "Yes, Miss Hoffman. Even the long ones."

"It's *Ms.* Hoffman," she corrected.

I didn't even have a chance to reply to that because then the book report interrogation began. I passed every question with flying colors—Napoleonic Wars, plot points, even obscure character drama. By the end, she dropped her arms and gave me a smile that nearly knocked me over.

"Well, color me impressed, Rockabilly. I had no idea you were that well-read."

"You never asked." Okay, I admit I was a little smug.

She shrugged. "You never acted like someone worth asking."

"Ouch."

She laughed again, and I found myself grinning like a dope.

"You used to pull my hair, remember?" she added.

"I was thirteen."

"You were a menace."

"Maybe. But I've changed."

"Have you?"

I met her gaze squarely. "No more hair pulling." Then I let my voice drop just enough. "Unless you want me to."

Her breath caught—just slightly—but it was enough.

And yeah. I was in trouble.

CHAPTER 9

Two seconds later — Ellie

Had Luke just flirted with me?

That grin—lazy, knowing, devastating—flashed across his face, and a jolt of heat zinged straight through me. Not the polite kind. The *knees-go-wobbly* kind.

Okay. Definitely flirting.

I did the only thing a semi-sane woman could do in that moment—I ignored him. Flat out. Pivoted away and started walking like I hadn't just had a full-body response to a five-word sentence.

"So, is that it for this floor?" I asked, forcing my voice to sound casual, not like I was mentally replaying the part where he offered to pull my hair.

He bit his lip. "Mostly. Plus the patio and backyard. Or, as the realtor insisted, 'the grounds.'"

I raised a brow. "How *expansive* are your grounds, Mr. Knightley?" I asked, giving it my best BBC-drama accent. Meg would've wheezed.

Luke winced, mock-humble. "Three and a half acres. Not *that* big. Just enough for privacy."

"Privacy," I echoed, following him through the sleek kitchen and out a set of French doors.

The patio looked like it belonged in a luxury resort—stone flooring, a full outdoor kitchen, massive TV, and a pool that could host Olympic trials. Black-and-white-striped umbrellas shaded lounge areas, and beyond that, manicured grass rolled into a cluster of trees.

"How far back does the land go?" I asked.

He gave a nonchalant shrug. "Far enough."

Just then, two dogs came bounding toward us—one golden retriever and one brown-and-white spaniel.

"And who are these good boys?" I crouched to greet them, instantly smitten.

"The golden is Huckleberry—Remington's. And this is Dolly. She's mine."

"Dolly?" I asked, scratching the spaniel behind her ears. She leaned into me like we'd known each other for years.

"Short for Dolly Parton. Legend. Icon. National treasure."

Okay. Cue the internal swoon I didn't ask for. I couldn't love Dolly Parton more.

We exchanged a smile, and I realized: Luke Knightley loved Dolly Parton too. This was…new data.

"Didn't I see two dog beds in the mudroom?" I asked.

"Yep. Built one in for Huck when Remington moved in. Dogs are family."

He said it like it was obvious, but my heart made an odd little stutter. Marie, my rescue mutt, had passed away last year, and I still wasn't over it. I hadn't expected Luke to be a dog person. Especially not *this* kind of dog person. The kind that commissions a bed for his *friend's* dog.

"Where'd you get Dolly?" I asked, assuming the answer would involve a breeder and a pedigree.

"Shelter. I asked who'd been there the longest."

Okay, wow. Heart somersault.

"She'd been returned a few times," he added, gently rubbing her side. "Behavioral stuff. But I told her she had a forever home with me if she wanted."

I *seriously* doubted my heart would survive this.

"I hired a trainer. Worth every penny." He looked down at her, smiling like she'd hung the moon. She gazed back at him like she agreed.

I swallowed the lump forming in my throat. "I'm glad she has you."

"I'm glad I have her," he said softly. "She's the only female I've managed to commit to."

I barked a laugh. "I wasn't going to say it."

"But you were thinking it?" he teased, one brow raised.

"Maybe." I gave him a look, but I was smiling too hard to sell it.

He winked again. And my stomach did a ridiculous, traitorous swoop.

Luke turned, gesturing toward the yard. "That's pretty much it. There's a half-court and tennis court somewhere out there, but it's a hike."

I followed him back inside, very aware that I was walking next to a man who'd saved a troubled shelter dog and loved Dolly Parton. Dangerous territory.

"So, how'd you like the tour?" he asked once we were back in the kitchen.

"It was—" I hesitated. "Wait. What about your bedroom?"

Luke's brow arched. "You want to see my bedroom?"

My mouth opened. "Not like *that*. Just—look, this place is insane. Your guest room is nicer than any hotel I've ever stayed in. I'm curious what the main suite looks like."

He grinned. "It's not *that* exciting."

I crossed my arms. "You have a chandelier that lowers on command. Show me the room."

"Fine. But only because you asked so nicely, Nurse Hoffman."

I followed him up the opposite staircase, through a wide hallway, and to a pair of massive double doors. He opened them—and yeah. It was ridiculous.

Vaulted ceilings, dark hardwoods, a bed big enough to get lost in. Shelves, a wall-mounted TV the size of a movie screen, and light flooding in from a wall of windows.

"It's huge," I said.

He smirked. "I hear that a lot in bedrooms."

I gave him a look. "Ha. Ha."

He gestured toward a door. "Bathroom's through there."

The bathroom looked like a spa married a five-star hotel. Gleaming marble. Double everything. A closet the size of my entire apartment.

I peeked inside—and immediately regretted it. Not because it wasn't amazing. But because I now knew Luke Knightley had a closet with color-coded rows of custom suits and a suitcase-packing station.

What even.

Then came the second closet. It was empty. I blinked.

"This one's for my partner," he said, rubbing the back of his neck.

"No groupies living in sin with you, huh?"

He winced. "Wow. Savage."

"Sorry. Old habits."

"Nah, it's fair. But no. This closet can stay empty for all I care."

I was about to reply with something kinda snarky, but I spotted the gauze on the counter. Right. I wasn't there to ogle his dream house—or appreciate his unexpectedly charming personality.

I turned to him. "How's your arm?"

He sighed. "Throbbing. I should probably change the bandage."

I stepped closer. "Where's the wound?"

"Right here." He pointed to a spot above his heart.

"Take off your shirt," I said, trying to stay clinical.

His grin was anything but clinical. "Yes, ma'am."

He unbuttoned his flannel one-handed like it was no big deal. And then…good lord.

He shrugged it off his shoulder, and there they were—six-pack abs, sculpted chest, and more muscle than should be legal. I blinked. Forgot what air was.

"Holy shit," I muttered.

"Like what you see?"

I was too stunned to answer. Had I ever seen him shirtless before? Surely. But *that*? That was…new.

"I've been working out," he added smugly.

"Noted," I said faintly.

He went to peel the gauze, and I slapped his hand away. "Let me."

I grabbed gloves, alcohol, and tape—pointedly ignoring the box of condoms the size of a small microwave. Not my business. I was there to change a dressing, not think about Luke's sex life.

I worked quickly, trying not to let my fingers linger on his skin. Or notice the line of hair trailing into his jeans. Or picture what kind of underwear he probably wore. (Boxer-briefs. Obviously.)

"It looks good," I said.

"I told you. I've been working out." His smile was devilish.

"I meant the wound," I lied. Mostly.

"It's healing well?"

"Pink and healthy. No signs of infection. I don't see why you need a full-time nurse."

He nodded, pulling his shirt back on. "The insurance company demands it."

"Shocking. Insurance is the devil. So egregious."

"That's what I like about you," he said.

"What, my intense hatred of bureaucracy?"

He gave me a crooked smile. "You say things like 'egregious.'"

I smirked. "Don't your groupies have vocabularies?"

His brow shot up. "You seem really fixated on the groupies."

I winced. "Sorry. I saw the condoms and jumped to conclusions."

He shrugged. "Safe sex is responsible. You should approve."

Touché.

"What if I told you I've never had a one-night stand?" he asked.

I laughed. Out loud.

"I'm serious."

I blinked. "You are?"

"I don't believe in them. I prefer to actually know someone. Spend some time. A few weeks, maybe months."

My brain short-circuited. That wasn't what I expected. At all. Luke Knightley had never had a one-night stand? Hard to believe. On the other hand, why would he lie about it? He had no reason to.

I quickly turned away and shoved the supplies back into the drawer—pointedly avoiding eye contact with the XXL Trojan box.

"What pain meds are you taking?" I asked.

"None."

I frowned. "None? At all?"

"Not risking addiction. Not after my dad."

The air shifted. Quiet. Serious. I knew all about his and

Meg's father. He'd battled more than one addiction. Alcohol. Gambling. Their mom had finally kicked him out. I didn't blame Luke for being wary.

I nodded. "Makes sense. I respect that."

"Thanks," he said, softly this time.

"Thanks for showing me your room," I added, matching his tone.

He smiled. "I'll walk you back."

"No need. I've got it."

At the door, I paused. "We should talk about the nursing position."

He shook his head. "Not yet."

I frowned. "What? Why not?"

He leaned against the doorframe. "Because first, you're letting me wine and dine you. Dinner. Eight o'clock."

The door clicked shut.

I walked back to my room in a daze.

Wine and dine me? He was *charming*. Disarming. And entirely too tempting.

And that was the problem.

CHAPTER 10

Twenty minutes later — Ellie

"Hey, I'm calling from Rich People Central," I said as soon as Gran picked up the phone. I dropped onto the edge of the giant guest bed and glanced around the room. "Luke's house looks like Martha Stewart and *Architectural Digest* had a baby."

"Any hanky-panky yet?"

I rolled my eyes and flopped backward onto the duvet. "Gran, I *just* got here."

"You know what they say. No time like the present."

I snorted. "I'm about to head down for dinner. No scandals—yet."

We chatted for a few more minutes. She'd taken her meds, still refused to touch her cell phone, and, according to her, she and Rosie had spent the afternoon trying to determine whether Mr. Hammond had a lady friend shacked up with him.

"He's been getting *mail* addressed to a Sylvia," she whispered like she was sharing state secrets.

I reminded her—again—that breaking and entering was still illegal.

"I wasn't breaking anything," she huffed. "Peeking in from the sidewalk is fair game. It's called *being observant*."

When we finally hung up, I was still smiling, head shaking, heart a little lighter. I sat up, pulled on a cream sweater and gray leggings, then checked my reflection in the mirror. Not too casual, not too interested. Perfect.

With a deep breath and fingers crossed for backup, I padded down the hallway toward the kitchen—quietly praying Meg and Jeremy were already there. Because more alone time with Luke? Dangerous territory.

After ogling his bare chest earlier, being alone with him now felt like playing with matches in a fireworks store. And despite whatever wining and dining he had in mind, I fully intended to decline his job offer. It was just too…much. Meg and I would be back on our way to Milwaukee tomorrow. Or the next day, max.

The kitchen smelled like roasted garlic and something buttery, rich, and spiced—comfort food with an edge. A woman I assumed was the private chef moved between two stoves. The rest of the room was empty.

She gave me a friendly smile. "Mr. Knightley should be back shortly. Can I get you a drink?"

Could she ever. "Yes, please. You're Linda, right?"

"That's me. What would you like, Ms. Hoffman?"

Oh, yeah. The staff was clearly briefed. "Pinot noir, if you've got it. And please call me Ellie."

She disappeared through a door that presumably led to the wine room, and I wandered toward the fireplace. Candles were lit in the hearth, vanilla and jasmine in the air—cozy, warm, inviting.

Linda returned with a deep red wine. "Here you go."

"Thanks. Smells divine."

She beamed. "Luke let me stock the cellar myself. I was in heaven."

I smiled, resisting the urge to ask what the wine room budget had been. I'd just ask Meg later. But another question was burning.

"What's it like working for Luke?"

"Honestly? He's one of the good ones. Low-key. Generous."

I blinked. "Generous?"

She lowered her voice, glancing around. "He paid for my son's surgery last year. Gabe was in a car accident. Luke covered the hospital bills and gave me paid time off. After that, he got health insurance for all the staff."

I stared at her. "You're serious?"

"He even let Gabe stay here to recover so I could look after him."

I managed a breath. "That's…incredible."

"Please don't tell him I told you," she said quickly. "He hates when people make a big deal out of it."

"My lips are sealed," I promised.

Footsteps sounded in the hallway, and I turned, silently chanting *Please let it be Meg.*

It was not Meg.

Luke strolled in with Dolly at his side—hair tousled, jeans slung low, the kind of casual confidence that should be illegal.

"Hey," he said, smiling like this was his kitchen in a life-style magazine. Which, okay, it basically was.

"Hey," I replied, trying to sound unfazed. Normal. Not like someone who'd recently been confronted by his abs.

Linda reappeared with a light beer for him, then quietly returned to the stove.

"Have you seen Meg and Jeremy?" I asked, wine glass clutched like a lifeline.

Luke scratched the back of his head. "Yeah…about that. They're not coming."

My stomach sank. "Why not?"

"They're, uh…busy." He gave me a knowing look.

I clamped my mouth shut. Yep. I knew exactly what that meant. And no, I couldn't be mad about it. Meg hadn't seen Jeremy in weeks. But that meant…

"It's just you and me for dinner," Luke added, exhaling.

Fantastic.

"Shall we?" He nodded toward the French doors.

I downed half my wine in one gulp and followed him outside. The patio looked like something out of a movie—white tablecloth, twinkling candles, fireplace crackling, roses in a crystal vase.

"This feels…romantic," I said before my brain could stop my mouth.

Luke grimaced. "I thought Meg and Jeremy would be joining us. Linda already reset the table."

"Right. Of course." Not romantic. *Not* a date. Just fancy, rich-people ambiance.

He pulled out my chair with his uninjured arm. I sat, still trying to convince myself this wasn't a mistake. Dolly curled up by the fire like she knew the vibes were suspiciously cozy.

"It's beautiful here," I said.

Luke chuckled. "Bit different than Twin Valley, huh?"

I met his eyes. "You've come a long way, Luke. It's impressive."

He looked down. "I just got lucky."

"No," I said. "I've heard your album. It's good. Really good."

His brows lifted. "You listened to it?"

"Of course. 'Summer Nights' is my favorite."

"Really?" His smile turned soft, almost shy. "You know I wrote that one in high school."

I blinked. "Seriously?"

"Yep. Tweaked it over the years, but the bones were there. The producers just gave it polish."

Before I could say more, Linda arrived with the first course: arugula salad, shaved parmesan, candied pecans, and cherry tomatoes. All my favorite things. I nearly hugged the plate.

"You eat like this every night?" I asked between bites.

Luke grinned. "No. Usually it's leftovers. I only ask Linda to stay when I have company."

Next came blackened salmon with mushroom risotto and crispy Brussels sprouts. I might've actually squealed.

"I *love* blackened salmon."

"I know," Luke said, lifting his glass in a toast. "Thanks to my sister."

I blinked. "You asked Meg about my food preferences?"

"I did my homework."

"And my guest room? The fact that it's decorated in my favorite color isn't a coincidence, is it?"

He shrugged, not even pretending to be sorry. "Periwinkle, right?"

"Wow." I shook my head. "Trying to impress me?"

"Is it working?"

"Does it work on the groupies?"

"Wow. You're really convinced I'm into groupies, huh?"

"You're not?"

"Not at all."

"Well, I've seen women show up to Meg's door begging to talk to you while you hid in the kitchen."

He winced. "Okay, guilty. But I never lied to anyone. I've just always been upfront—short-term fun only. No hard feelings."

"Does that work?"

"Sometimes. Sometimes…not so much."

I thought of Vance, my ex, and his collection of lies and excuses. Luke might have been a serial dater, but he was honest about it. And somehow, that felt…different.

"So you think I'm a player?" he asked, eyebrow cocked.

"I mean…" I paused, chewing slowly. "Kind of?"

"At least I'm not deceptive," he said, reaching for his drink. "And I don't ghost."

"Well, that's more than I can say for a lot of men."

He smiled, then set his glass down and looked at me seriously. "What do you think?"

I frowned. "About what?"

"About the job. Staying here."

Ah. There it was. Wining, dining, and now the pitch.

I pushed risotto around on my plate. "I appreciate the offer, but I really can't. I'm not a home health nurse. It's not what I do."

"But you *are* qualified. And you can take some time off from the hospital, right?"

Now how did he know that? *Meg.*

"I'm volunteering with the Children's Hospital. Planning the summer gala."

"You can do all of that here," he said. "Phone calls, Zoom meetings—whatever. You'd only need to check my arm, change the gauze, fill out some forms for the insurance company."

"And the days I need to be in Milwaukee?"

"The jet's yours whenever you need it."

I stared at him. The *jet*? Sexy. Distracting. But not a dealmaker.

"I don't get it," I said. "You could hire anyone. Why me?"

Luke's jaw tightened. His voice dropped. "Because I don't know who I can trust right now."

I blinked. That vulnerability wasn't a vibe I was used to from him. And yet…I recognized it.

"I understand. Meg told me what happened with the last nurse—"

"It's not just that. It's everything. Fame. Money. Suddenly people act different. Even in my own house, I don't know who's real anymore."

A long beat passed.

I reached out, meaning to offer simple reassurance, but the second my hand touched his, heat surged up my arm. I pulled away quickly.

He noticed.

"I'm not asking you to do this for me," he said. "Do it for the kids. I'll donate the entire $250,000 to the hospital if you stay."

I nearly knocked over my wine glass. "You'd *what*?" How did he know that was the exact amount I was trying to raise? He'd done his homework, indeed.

"I'll donate it either way," he added quickly. "But I'm asking you to stay…as a friend."

My heart punched my ribs. He was serious. Sincere.

"Why is it so important?" I asked, voice quiet.

He exhaled. "Because I trust you, Ellie. And right now, that's rare."

Damn it.

My brain screamed *danger.* But my heart? My heart was already sliding the scale from "hell no" to "maybe." And that was the most dangerous part of all.

CHAPTER 11

Later Sunday night — Ellie

"*Sleep on it? Please,*" Luke had said before I came upstairs. But the second he'd said, "*Do it for the children,*" I knew it was over. What was I supposed to do—say no to a man who offered to donate an obscene amount of money to a children's hospital and asked me to stay with the wide-eyed sincerity of a rescue dog?

If he'd been even a little smug, or implied I'd say yes for the money, I could've packed my righteous indignation and flown home first thing tomorrow. But no. He played the *earnest and emotionally vulnerable* card. Damn him.

But the real reason I was staying?

Luke Knightley—childhood adversary, grown-up temptation, and newly-revealed softie—had looked me straight in the eye and asked for my help. *As a friend.* And apparently, I'm a sucker for sincerity in a six-foot-one, muscled, guitar-playing package.

He'd been open. Honest. He trusted me. He'd even offered the jet so I could still see Mindy—though let's be real, I would switch to video calls for the environment, not because a private jet wasn't absurdly tempting.

I had the time. I had the skills. And if I said no, I'd feel like a garbage friend.

Were there at least six reasons why this was a terrible idea? Absolutely.

Reason one: Luke was hot.

Reason two: Luke was charming.

Reason three through six? We were going to be under the same roof, with nothing but unresolved tension and shared history to keep things interesting.

But technically, I was here in a professional capacity. Not to revisit old fantasies. Not to notice how his shirts stretched across his biceps. Not to fall into anything resembling a crush.

I'd stay in my lane. Do my job. Avoid him when possible. The house had about forty-seven rooms. And Meg and Jeremy were here. Luke and I would barely even see each other. It was fine. Totally manageable.

A soft knock interrupted my mental *Do Not Lust Over the Patient* lecture.

I opened the door to find Meg, looking both sheepish and slightly flushed.

"Missed you at dinner," I said, stepping back.

She smiled guiltily. "Yeah...sorry. I heard there was blackened salmon?"

"There was. It was amazing."

She walked in and dropped onto the edge of the bed. "So...Luke kind of sent me to check the odds."

Classic Meg—terrible liar, didn't even try. One of her better qualities. She wasn't here to check the odds. She was here to push me across the finish line. Get me to say yes.

I sat beside her with a sigh, crossing my arms. "Did he

happen to mention he offered to donate *two hundred and fifty grand* to the children's hospital if I agree to stay?"

Meg's jaw dropped. "He did *what?*"

I nodded slowly. "Yup."

"Holy crap. No, he didn't mention that."

"Yeah, well, he did." I sighed.

Meg grinned. "You should let him do it. He spent nearly that much on the couches."

"I'm not stopping him. But I'll admit, I'm shocked he's this determined to have *me* be his nurse. Up until about four days ago, I thought he couldn't stand me."

"I told you," she said, bumping my shoulder. "That's just Luke. He gives hell to the people he likes."

"You sure? Because I'm pretty sure he used to go out of his way to annoy me."

"Exactly."

I rolled my eyes but…yeah. He hadn't given me hell since I got here. In fact, I'd been the one dishing it out, and he'd been meeting me with sincerity. That was the confusing part. We were… What? Becoming actual friends? Real ones?

Meg's voice softened. "He's really worried, Ellie. I think he needs you."

I glanced down at my socks on the plush rug and blew out a long breath.

"Yeah," I said quietly. "I got that too."

Meg leaned in. "So…you're staying?"

I stood, hands on hips, and nodded. "I'm staying."

Her face lit up. "Awesome. Let's go tell him. He's gonna be thrilled."

Monday morning — Luke

Last night, when Ellie told me she was staying, the relief hit so hard I nearly dropped to my knees.

What had started as a solid idea—hire someone I trust—had turned into something I couldn't let go of. I wasn't even entirely sure why. I just knew that with her in the house, I felt…safer. Calmer. Like I could exhale for the first time in weeks.

That didn't mean it wasn't complicated.

She was beautiful. Obviously. And I was technically her boss now, which meant I needed to lock that attraction in a box, bury it in the yard, and forget the coordinates. No flirting. No feelings. Just clean bandages and professional boundaries.

I'd already called my manager, Mark, to tell him the good news. The insurance company would finally get off my back. He said the paperwork was on the way and immediately asked about an NDA. I told him it wasn't necessary. When he pushed, I shut him down.

"I trust her," I said. "That's the whole point."

After the logistics were settled and Dolly was snoring softly in her bed, I opened my laptop for my weekly virtual therapy session with Dr. Heinselberg. Dr. H, as I'd taken to calling her, was one of those wildly calm, almost unnerving professionals you could throw any emotional chaos at and she'd still blink like, *Go on.*

I'd started therapy after the last nurse sold the photos of me to a tabloid. After it had all gone viral, Mark insisted I talk to someone before I became a full-blown recluse.

Spoiler alert: I already kind of had.

It's not like I didn't leave the house at all. I just didn't want to. Not when there could be a camera hiding in a shrub. Which sounds paranoid—until you wake up one day as a meme.

Dr. H didn't pry too much. Yet. But I knew the past was coming. The dad stuff. The addiction stuff. The endless second-guessing of anyone's motives once you hit a certain net worth. Fun times.

This morning, she asked how things were going. I told her about Ellie. Told her I'd finally found someone I trusted enough to let inside the walls—literal and metaphorical.

She didn't say much. Just encouraged me, again, to leave the house this week. Go anywhere. Do anything.

"Exposure therapy," she called it. "Go toward the discomfort."

"Yeah, sure," I muttered. "I'll get right on that."

When our session ended, I shut the laptop and tapped the remote. The security feed popped up on the big screen, split into a dozen views of the property. A black SUV pulled into the driveway. Meg and Ellie were back from the shopping trip I'd sent them on with my credit card. Ellie hadn't packed much when she came—just a few things, expecting to leave in a day or two. I wanted to make sure she didn't need to.

Not because of the clothes.

Because if she left, she might not come back.

I fired off a quick email to my bandmates about our weekly Zoom call and rehearsing later in the week, then stood when I heard a knock at the door.

When I opened it, Ellie was there wearing the same sweater and leggings from last night.

Damn. Those leggings were a problem.

"Hey," she said, smiling.

I tried not to stare. Or think. Or imagine things I really, really shouldn't be imagining about someone who worked for me.

"Find some clothes?"

"Yeah, thank you," she said, reaching down to ruffle Dolly's ears. "I didn't go crazy—just a few staples. Mostly new underwear."

Oh, *perfect.* Now I had mental images I absolutely did not need. I cleared my throat.

"Well, you can always get more if you need anything," I said, stepping aside to let her in.

"Thanks." She moved past me, all business. "I filled out the paperwork you sent this morning. And according to the terms, I need to treat your wound every twenty-four hours."

She tapped her watch. "It's time."

"Right. Of course."

She walked straight into the bathroom, already pulling out the gauze and alcohol like she'd been doing this for years. Which, to be fair, she had.

"Shirt off," she said, not looking at me.

I tugged the fabric over my head and stepped closer. She finally glanced up, her gaze locking onto my shoulder like it was the only part of me in the room. Her hands were steady as she peeled back the bandage, but her eyes flicked downward once—just once—and I saw the quick swallow.

She focused again. "Still looks good."

I wanted to crack another joke about my workout routine, but I kept it in. I was trying to behave. And this was not the time to flirt with someone who had both medical gloves and access to alcohol swabs.

She dabbed the wound with practiced ease. I hissed softly, more from the contact than the sting. Her fingers brushed against my skin, gentle and professional. But I felt every damn second of it.

I shifted my weight, hoping to God she didn't notice the situation in my pants. Because if she thought for even a second that I was getting off on this, she'd bolt.

Ellie replaced the gauze, smoothed down the tape, and finally stepped back. "You're lucky the wound wasn't a few inches lower."

"Tell me about it."

I caught her gaze for half a second. There was heat there. Or maybe I imagined it. Either way, I couldn't act on it. Not now.

She cleared her throat and started packing up the supplies. I grabbed my shirt and tried to force my brain to reset.

This was fine. We were fine. I could do professional.

Even if she was standing in my bathroom, smelling like warm vanilla and looking like temptation in leggings.

Even if every instinct I had told me that this—*this*—was going to get a whole lot harder before it got easier.

CHAPTER 13

Monday night — Ellie

I t started off badly. Meg and Jeremy had to fly back to Milwaukee. Health emergency with Mrs. Timms, Jeremy's elderly next door neighbor, who was like a second mother to him. They took the private jet.

After they left, I tried to fill the day with anything that didn't involve thinking about Luke. I'd already emailed Lena last night to tell her I'd be taking time off work. She replied with one word: "Hallelujah."

After checking in with Gran again and getting an earful of sass, I hit the basement gym, made a dozen calls about the charity gala, and mentally replayed the moment when I'd treated Luke's wound and had practically begun drooling.

Now it was dinner time, and I was low-key dreading it. Would it be weird? Was I going to think about Luke's shoulders the entire meal? Probably yes to all of the above.

And with Meg and Jeremy gone, the air in the house felt different. Quieter. Closer.

I reminded myself why I was here: *Two hundred and fifty*

thousand dollars. For the kids. That was the mantra. Not "Luke's aftershave smells amazing" or "I wonder what his face look like when he sleeps." Just: *For the kids.*

I made my way downstairs.

Linda was nowhere to be seen when I walked into the kitchen, but Luke was there—perched on a barstool at one of the islands, laptop open, Dolly curled up near the fireplace like a sleepy guardian angel.

He looked up, and his face lit up with a smile so effortless and warm it made my pulse trip over itself.

"Hey," I said, tugging on my ring finger like the nervous tic that it was.

"Hey," he replied, slipping his hand into his jeans pocket. Casual. Friendly. Ridiculously attractive.

Something was different. "Did you get a haircut?" I asked.

"Yeah. Had my barber swing by."

"Your barber makes *house calls?*"

He grinned. "Doesn't yours?"

I rolled my eyes but smiled. Of course Luke had a traveling barber. Probably showed up complete with a leather case and a straight-edge razor.

I leaned on the island, trying to sound breezy. "So, what does a country rock star do all day when he's grounded?"

Luke tipped his head back and forth. "Write lyrics. Mess around in the studio. *Wish* I could play guitar."

I wrinkled my nose. "Sounds...productive."

"You hungry?"

"Always."

Luke pulled two plates from the fridge—both covered like room service. He revealed pasta shells in marinara, then grabbed two little bowls of cheese from the fridge.

"Linda left instructions. Parmesan *and* pecorino. No shortcuts."

"As it should be," I said solemnly. We were Wisconsinites. Cheese was practically a religion.

He slid the first plate into the microwave and hit Start. "Three minutes exactly. Linda would disown me if I messed it up."

"She's got good boundaries."

He gave a quiet laugh. "Yeah."

Something flickered across his face then. Thoughtful. Sad.

"What?" I asked.

He ran a hand through his freshly cut hair. "I was just thinking about my mom. I wish she'd let me help her."

I tilted my head. "What stops her?"

He gave a half-shrug, gaze distant. "Pride, maybe. Or habit. She's always been the type to patch things with duct tape and call it resilience. When I offered to pay off her mortgage, she told me it was none of my business."

"That's harsh."

"She didn't mean it like that," he said quickly. "She just… doesn't know how to accept help without feeling small. And I don't know how to show her it's not charity. It's just love. And don't even ask about the time I offered to buy her a new house."

He rubbed the back of his neck, his voice quieter now. "Sometimes I think she still sees me as the kid with a guitar and no clue what he was doing."

"You can't force someone to accept help," I said.

"I know. But it doesn't stop me from wanting to."

I nodded, and we let the moment breathe.

When the microwave dinged, he swapped plates and nodded toward the French doors. "Want to eat outside again?"

"Actually…can we just eat here?"

He blinked, then smiled. "Absolutely. This is where I eat most of the time anyway."

"Me too—at my place. Usually standing over the sink with a frozen dinner."

"Which is why pizza is the perfect food," he said. "It turns dinner into a party."

A few minutes later, we were seated at the kitchen island, sharing cheese, passing basil, sipping wine (me) and beer (him), and—shockingly—enjoying a totally normal meal.

"This is delicious," I said between bites.

"Yeah. Linda's the real rock star in this house."

I tilted my head. "How does someone even get a private chef anyway?"

Luke shrugged. "Honestly? You don't. You get money, and suddenly people show up to help you spend it."

I laughed. "Fair enough."

After we finished eating, he stood and dropped the dishes into the dishwasher without ceremony. I was about to excuse myself when he gestured toward the sitting area.

"Want to hang out for a bit? Couch time?"

Of course, it would've been easier to say no. Safer, at least. But the thing about awkward tension was that ignoring it only made it grow. Pretending we were normal felt… easier. So I nodded. "Sure."

"Bring your wine," he said.

I hesitated. "I can't drink red wine on a couch that expensive."

He looked at me like I hadn't spoken English. "What?"

"Meg told me how much that couch cost. If I spill—"

He shrugged. "I'll just have it cleaned."

"What if it *doesn't* come out?"

Another shrug. "Then I'll have a wine-stained couch. Come on."

I followed, clutching my glass like a bomb. I sat carefully on the very edge of the cushion and set my wine on the side table. Luke sat next to me, not too close, but not distant either.

He stretched out, his bare feet propped on the coffee table. Even his *feet* were attractive. Okay. I officially needed to go on a real date when I got home. Or maybe just get laid. Anything to reset this Luke-induced brain fog. And foot admiration? Just weird.

"What did you say?" he asked.

Oh God. "Nothing," I replied way too fast.

He turned, eyes narrowing. "Did you just say you need a date?"

My face lit on fire. "Maybe." Oh, crap. Had I said that out loud?

"You're single?" he asked, looking entirely too delighted by that revelation.

"Very," I said, staring straight ahead.

"'Very' as in...?" I could see his eyes narrow from the corner of mine.

"As in I haven't dated seriously in a long time," I breathed. Wow. That felt pretty heavy to say out loud.

His brow rose. "How long?"

I blew out a breath. "Since college."

He blinked. "College?"

I closed my eyes briefly. I never liked talking about this. "I was engaged. He cheated. End of story."

Luke's expression darkened. "You were *engaged*?"

I lifted one shoulder. "Briefly. Senior year. Meg probably never told you."

"No, she didn't." He shook his head, scowling. "He cheated? What a dick."

"Thanks," I said, lips twitching.

Luke leaned forward. "Wait, so you haven't dated since then?"

"A little bit. There were a few guys. Nothing serious."

He clutched his chest dramatically. "Thank God. I was about to stage an intervention."

I laughed. "You still can."

"What happened to the dick?" he asked next.

I laughed. "He's divorced now, I hear. From the woman he cheated on me with."

Luke shook his head. "Shocking."

"I know, right? I have a type. Or had one. I'm working on that."

His brows shot up. "Therapy?"

I took another gulp of wine. "Yup. Off and on. It's helped." Why were we talking about this again?

"I'm in therapy too," he said, almost sheepishly.

That surprised me more than it should have. "Really?"

He bobbed his head slowly. "Trying to untangle some stuff."

"Good for you," I said. And I meant it. I'd always seen it as a green flag when a man was willing to go to therapy.

A smile popped to his lips. "I mean, I'm still a mess, but I'm trying."

We fell quiet for a moment, the fire crackling in the background.

"So," he said, stretching again, "why haven't you gone out with anyone lately?"

Oh, no. We'd already talked enough about me. Time for some good, old-fashioned deflection. "What about you? Why are *you* single? It's not like there's a shortage of willing women."

He raised a brow. "You saying I have a reputation?"

"I'm saying you've *always* had a reputation. Since high school."

He laughed. "That tracks. But the truth is, I'm crap at relationships. I can start them just fine—it's keeping them that's the problem."

"And marriage? Kids? Are those not in the cards for you?"

He shook his head. "I don't think so. I know myself. I'd be a terrible father."

My heart ached a little at the certainty in his voice. But I guessed it was because his own father had been such a mess. "That's really sad, Luke."

He looked at me. "Maybe. But I'd rather be honest."

"What about you?" he asked. "You still want that? A family?"

"Yeah," I said softly. "If I can find the right guy. Not a liar. Not a cheater." I shrugged. "That narrows the pool."

He nodded again. "You deserve someone solid."

"Yeah?" I took another sip of wine. "You got any more friends like Jeremy lying around?"

"A couple. My bandmates are coming over later this week. I'll introduce you."

I raised a brow. "Are they hot and stable?"

He grinned. "Define stable. I don't know about hot."

The silence between us shifted then—tilted slightly into something heavier. He moved a little closer, eyes serious. "Ellie…thank you. For staying. I know you didn't have to, and I really appreciate it."

His gaze dipped to my mouth. Oh God. He was going to kiss me.

Panic hit. I leaped off the couch like it was on fire.

"Yep! Totally happy to help! Gotta go… Spreadsheets for the gala!"

I bolted out of the room and didn't stop until I hit the staircase.

Professional. I was going to be professional, dammit.

Even if the temptation was sitting barefoot on a hundred-thousand-dollar couch.

CHAPTER 14

Tuesday morning — Luke

I used to have game. Not like sleazy lines or anything, but at least a baseline understanding of how to read the room.

Apparently, that skill had officially left the building—because last night? Not smooth.

I'd leaned in. Maybe, possibly, sort of considering kissing Ellie. I wasn't even fully committed to the idea. But she didn't wait to find out. The second she sensed what might be coming, she shot off the couch like it was about to explode.

And I wasn't even offended. Mostly, I just felt like an idiot.

I knew she wasn't looking for a guy like me—she literally said so minutes before I almost kissed her. She wanted someone steady. Loyal. Safe. I might be loyal, but steady? That was generous. And watching her perk up at the idea of me introducing her to my single bandmates?

Let's just say I didn't love it.

Not jealousy, exactly. I didn't have a claim on her. But

something about it didn't sit right. Maybe it was that I liked having her here more than I should. Maybe I'd read too much into her laughing at my jokes or the way she looked at me sometimes. Or maybe I'd let the quiet house and my own loneliness mess with my head.

Either way, message received. I wasn't going to make that mistake again.

But part of me still wondered—should I say something? Apologize? Or would acknowledging it make things even more awkward?

I was still chewing on that when I heard her knock on the open door to my room.

Dolly leapt up and ran to her like she'd been gone for weeks. Ellie bent to greet her, dressed in all black—leggings and a fitted sweater—looking criminally good for a Tuesday morning.

"Ready?" she asked, straightening and brushing hair from her face like last night had never happened.

I stared at her like an idiot. "Ready for what?"

"The dressing," she said. "It's time."

Right. Of course. The reason she was here.

I nodded, pulled myself together, and followed her into the bathroom.

She washed her hands, all brisk efficiency, and pulled out the supplies like she was clocking in for work.

I peeled off my shirt again, and sat still as she pulled on gloves and cleaned the wound, reapplied gauze, and taped me up like I was her most boring patient of the day.

It was over in seconds.

"Ellie, look—"

But she spoke before I could figure out what to say next.

"How did you find out?" she asked quietly, her voice softer now. "About the last nurse? The pictures?"

I froze. Of all the conversations I'd expected, this wasn't it.

"You don't have to talk about it," she added quickly. "I understand if you'd rather not."

"No, it's okay." I took a breath. "My therapist says I should talk about it more, actually."

Ellie nodded and leaned against the counter, arms crossed loosely as she waited.

"It was after a band rehearsal," I began, eyes drifting to the trees outside the window behind her. "I was heading upstairs, checking my phone, and I saw a text from my manager. Just a link and three words: 'WTF is this?'"

Her face tightened in sympathy.

"I opened it. It was a tabloid site with a picture of me—mouth open, asleep in bed. Nothing horrible at first, just... personal. Too personal. Then more pictures. Me in the shower. Shirtless in bed. A whole collection. The story was already blowing up."

"And you knew it was her?" Ellie asked.

"Yeah. I mean, who else could it have been? No one else had been in my room."

She gave me a look.

"Not like *that*," I said. "She was a nurse. It was professional. I swear."

"I believe you," Ellie said, nodding.

"She packed up and left before I even saw the article. Probably tipped off by the tabloid. Gone without a trace."

"Damn," she murmured.

"The next day, my manager came over and we started damage control. Lawsuits, threats, PR spin. But it was already out there. Can't unring that bell."

"I'm so sorry, Luke," Ellie said. "That's...an incredible violation. She'll lose her license for that, I hope you know. Nurses take confidentiality seriously."

"Yeah. Doesn't exactly undo it though."

"No. It doesn't."

I exhaled hard and rubbed a hand across my jaw. "Fame's got its perks. But I never thought I'd need an NDA for my own house. And now? I'm pretty much a mental disaster."

Ellie didn't say anything for a long moment. Then she reached out and rested her hand on my right shoulder.

"You're not a disaster, Luke. You're a guy who's been through something really crappy."

I swallowed against the lump in my throat. Coming from her, it hit different. Like it counted more.

"What does your therapist suggest?" she asked gently, pulling her hand back.

I wrinkled my nose. "Uh…she wants me to leave the house." Wow. Saying it out loud like that made it sound so dumb.

Ellie's brows lifted. "Leave… Like actually go somewhere?"

"Yeah. Around town. Baby steps."

Ellie nodded. "Well, she's right."

I took a breath. It was now or never. "Will you come with me?"

Her eyes widened. "Me?"

"Yeah." I scratched the back of my neck, hoping I sounded as nonchalant as I meant to. "Just lunch or something. It'd help to not do it alone."

Her brows drew together. "You don't have friends who could go with you?"

I met her gaze. "I do. But I want *you.* I don't know why exactly. Maybe because I've known you so long. It's just… easier around you."

She looked like she was debating a dozen ways to say no. I didn't blame her. How could I? I already asked a lot of her, and now I was asking for more.

"Please?" I added, because apparently I was officially pathetic now.

She let out a slow breath. "Okay. But it's gotta be burgers. No caviar, no fire-roasted figs, or anything that needs to be cooked with a blowtorch. Casual."

I grinned. "Deal."

CHAPTER 15

An hour later — Ellie

The Range Rover pulled up behind a place called *Burger Up*—hip and rustic-looking, with enough wood and black metal to feel Nashville-trendy. I was hoping for nothing more than a killer burger and a break from the tension simmering under my skin.

On the way over, I tried to focus on the scenery, the weather, literally anything other than Luke beside me in the car, looking gorgeous and more nervous than I'd ever seen him. The night before, I'd convinced myself I hadn't *really* fled from an almost-kiss. Maybe he'd just leaned in a little. Maybe I'd overreacted. But I'd still ended the night hiding under my comforter chanting "strictly business" like a mantra and dreaming about kissing him anyway. Ugh.

Today, I'd shown up at his bedroom door in full Nurse Mode—clipped tone, brisk movements, no eye contact. And he'd matched the energy. Then I'd derailed us both by asking about his former nurse and the whole betrayal bombshell. But to his credit, Luke had opened up. And once again, I'd been reminded of the complicated, wounded guy hiding behind the charm. Not that it excused the way he made my stomach flip or my brain short-circuit when he looked at me with those eyes.

The car rolled to a stop behind the restaurant. Apparently, celebrities didn't go through the front entrance like the rest of us. One of the security guys opened my door.

"You okay?" I asked Luke.

He swallowed hard and nodded. "Yeah. Let's do it."

To my surprise, he reached for my hand. Just a quick squeeze. But it sent a ripple of warmth through me. His grip was solid, a little sweaty. Understandable. Two bodyguards flanked us as we hustled through the kitchen and into a small private dining room.

"VIP life," I said, glancing around. It was charming and cozy, like a speakeasy with better lighting.

"Most restaurants have private rooms, it turns out," Luke said, pulling out my chair with one arm. "One of the perks of fame. That and always getting your drinks right."

I laughed as the waitress arrived and handed us menus—along with our drinks, already poured. "Let me guess. Your people called ahead?"

He gave a sheepish nod. "I think they texted."

We both ordered burgers and fries, and when we were alone again, I said, "You're brave, you know."

He raised an eyebrow.

"Coming here. Trusting the staff. Putting yourself back out in the world."

His jaw flexed. "It pisses me off, honestly. What Tiffany did—I hate how much it messed with me. I don't want to be the guy who hides forever. I want to feel like myself again."

I nodded slowly. "I get that."

He looked at me like he was trying to read my thoughts. "You thinking about your ex?"

I blinked. "Vance? Maybe."

Luke leaned in a little. "You let that guy steal your trust, Ellie. That's not fair to you."

My chest tightened. "You let someone take yours too."

He tipped his chin. "Which is why I'm here."

I smiled. "Then we should celebrate."

He arched a brow. "With?"

"Tequila shots." I waggled my eyebrows while Gran's voice rang in my head.

He laughed. "It's noon."

"All the better. We're not driving. We have nothing else to do. Consider it physical therapy."

So we did. We downed top-shelf tequila like college kids, licked limes, and laughed until my cheeks hurt. Luke's eyes sparkled, the kind of sparkle that made it *very* hard to remember that I was his nurse.

"I gotta say," he said after the burn faded, "I had you pegged wrong."

"Oh?"

He leaned his elbow on the table. "I used to think you had…a stick up your ass. No offense."

I barked a laugh. "None taken. And you weren't wrong."

He tilted his head. "So why was it there?"

I paused. Then shrugged. "Maybe because I grew up knowing I'd have to take care of my grandma. I needed to be the responsible one. Grades. Goals. Plans. I didn't have the luxury of screwing around."

Luke sat up straighter. "Damn. That's…a lot."

"Yeah. But she's good now. I moved her into a duplex near her church. She plays bingo every Wednesday and tells her neighbors about the 'rock star' I know."

He smiled, but it was sad around the edges. "Meg and I don't see our mom much. And we haven't heard from our dad in years."

"I know," I said simply. "I'm sorry."

Just then, the burgers arrived—massive, messy, and perfect. We dug in, and for a few minutes, we didn't talk. Just good food and easy silence.

And then the door slammed open.

A girl burst in, eyes wide. "Oh my God. Is Luke Knightley really in here?!"

One of the guards caught her before she could get more than a few steps. But she'd already spotted him.

"Luke! Please! Sign my *butt cheek*! I want to get it tattooed!"

Luke gave her a tight, practiced smile. "Just trying to enjoy a quiet lunch."

The guards escorted her out and shut the doors, muffling the chaos outside.

I turned to him with wide eyes. "That…happen a lot?"

He winced. "More than I'd like."

No kidding. The world didn't see Luke Knightley, the guy who worried about his mom and paid for his chef's son's surgery. They saw a fantasy. A headline. A rock star worth screaming for.

Which is why I needed to remember—no matter how sweet or sincere he was being—he wasn't mine to want. Not really.

The man had women who wanted his name tattooed on their *butt cheeks*, for God's sake.

And I needed to make damn sure I didn't fall for him.

CHAPTER 16

Tuesday late afternoon — Luke

The minute we got home from lunch, Ellie had hustled up to her room, and I hadn't seen her since. I didn't blame her. After the scene at lunch, anyone would need a break. The look on her face after that girl burst into the private room—wide eyes, tense jaw—told me she'd been rattled. She wasn't used to the kind of madness that came with a number-one album. Hell, I wasn't used to it either, but at least I'd stopped being shocked.

Since the record blew up, I'd had people camped outside my house, slipping notes under the gate, trying to scale the fence. One woman climbed in through a damn window. That's when I installed full security. Now they mostly showed up at the venues. But I knew the energy they carried —loud, intense, uninvited. And I knew it had shaken Ellie.

I ate some pretzels at the kitchen island, alone, the sports channel droning in the background. Getting out today had been a milestone, but it wasn't enough. I couldn't go back on tour still half-paralyzed by paranoia.

I pulled open my laptop. I had a call scheduled with my bandmates. It would be good to see the guys.

One minute later — Ellie

I STEPPED into the kitchen just as Luke's laptop started buzzing with a FaceTime call labeled *The Dangerous Idiots*.

I raised a brow. "Do I even want to know?"

Luke groaned. "It's the band."

I was already running my fingers through my hair. "Excellent. Time to determine their hotness level."

"Ellie—"

Too late. I answered.

Three faces popped up on the screen, all talking at once.

"—look alive, Nashville's own brooding heartthrob has entered the chat!"

"Is that the new nurse? Damn, she's real?"

"Oh, thank God. Someone competent."

Luke dragged a hand down his face. "Why do I let you have my number?"

The top left square showed *Wentworth*, dark hair closely shaved, scruffy beard, aviator glasses perched halfway down his nose like he'd just emerged from a recording dungeon.

Next to him was *Dashwood*, all dimples and leather bomber jacket, eating from a takeout container like it was a competitive sport.

Holt, in a vintage band tee and eyeliner with a messy bun, gave me a mock salute. "You must be Ellie."

I gave them all a wide smile. "I am. And you must be the chaos I've been warned about."

Holt grinned. "Oh, she's quick. I like her."

"What're y'all up to?" Luke quickly interjected.

"Glad you asked," Dashwood said, wiping his mouth. "We're going out. Just a chill night. Couple drinks. Live set at the Ryman afterparty."

Holt leaned into the camera. "And we want Ellie to come."

I blinked. "Me?"

"Of course," Wentworth said. "Anyone who survived the Knightley Recovery Ranch deserves a medal. And a drink."

Luke stiffened. "She's not going to a bar with you degenerates."

Dashwood smirked. "Protective. Cute."

Wentworth chimed in. "Come on. It's low-key. No press. Just a few industry folks and overpriced drinks."

Ellie looked between them. "Actually…I wouldn't mind going."

Luke's head snapped to me. "What?"

I shrugged. "It might be fun." Plus, if I didn't mistake my guess, Luke wasn't about to let me go alone, and he needed to get out more.

Luke's jaw clenched.

Wentworth caught it. "Come with, Knightley. Just for an hour."

"I don't—" Luke started, then stopped. I saw the flicker of panic, the calculation behind his eyes. The tension in his chest that had nothing to do with his injury.

He didn't like crowds. Or attention. Or the outside world that kept reminding him he was once unbreakable and now…not.

"Look," I said under my breath, turning to him so the others wouldn't hear. "You don't have to go. I'll be fine."

But that was the wrong thing to say. Or the right thing to say, depending on how I looked at it.

Luke sat up straighter. "Like hell you're going out with them without me."

Dashwood looked amused. "Didn't take you for the jealous type, Knightley."

"I'm not," Luke snapped. "I just know what you three are like in public."

I smothered a laugh.

Holt held up his hands. "No ulterior motives. Just company."

Luke still hesitated, and for a second, I thought he'd say no. But then he met my gaze, and something shifted. Determination. Maybe defiance. Maybe something else.

He looked back at the screen. "We'll see you guys at nine."

*FOUR HOURS LATER — **Ellie***

I needed to get downstairs to meet Luke, but first a quick call to Gran was in order.

"Oh good," she said when she answered. "You don't sound murdered."

"Close. I was ambushed by fangirls earlier."

"Were you wearing clean underwear?"

"Gran."

"Just checking. What happened?"

I filled her in, and she clucked like a mother hen. "Fame is loud, bean. Don't let it drown you out."

Wow. Gran had a knack for slipping real wisdom in between all the sass.

"Okay, gotta go. Call you tomorrow?"

"Sure. Just make sure it's not during *Wheel*."

"Promise."

I hurried downstairs and was sitting on one of the fancy couches when Luke emerged from the kitchen staircase wearing dark jeans, a black Henley, and a scowl.

I stood.

"Don't look at me like that," he muttered as I gave him an exaggerated once-over.

"I'm just impressed," I said. "You clean up almost too well for someone who used to eat pizza and sleep on Meg's couch."

He quirked a brow. "Remind me why I agreed to this?"

"Because you hate the idea of me alone with your friends." I gave him a huge smile. "It's not too late, you know? I can still go alone."

"No way." He held out his right hand. "Come on, Nurse. Let's go cause a scene."

I smiled to myself as he escorted me toward the door. I couldn't help being more than a little proud. Operation Get-Luke-Out-of-the-House-Twice-in-One-Day was a success. So far.

CHAPTER 17

Thirty minutes later — Ellie

The second we walked in, I got it.

Why Luke had hesitated. Why he'd stayed home for weeks. Why his jaw was tight and his hand brushed my back like he needed confirmation I hadn't vanished.

It wasn't the crowd—it was the way they looked at him.

Not loud. Not screaming. Just…a shift. Like gravity had tilted slightly toward us the moment we stepped through the door. Phones subtly angled. Heads turning. Curious whispers.

The security guards hung back. They were low-key, discreet. But I was glad to know they were there, just in case.

I leaned in. "You okay?"

Luke nodded once, but his eyes didn't stop scanning the room. "Just don't leave my side."

"Trust me," I said, looping my arm through his right arm. "Not planning on getting lost in here."

Christopher Wentworth spotted us first and waved us

toward the back booth, where he and Nick Holt were already halfway through a round. Liam Dashwood was chatting up the bartender with dimples that should've been illegal.

Luke had told me their first names on the ride over. He also informed me that all three of them were single. Because of course, I asked.

"Look who showed," Christopher said, raising his glass. "Knightley in the wild. Didn't think you'd actually do it."

Luke slid into the booth stiffly, keeping his slinged arm guarded. "I have no idea why I came."

"Because your nurse is hot," Nick said matter-of-factly, winking at me.

I blinked. "That's…not how HIPAA works."

Liam rejoined us with another round and a grin. "We ordered you a bourbon, Ellie. And something fruity for Luke. Maybe a spritz."

Luke glared. "You're hilarious."

"You love us."

"I tolerate you."

The drinks arrived, and for a while, the conversation spun into tour stories and band gossip. Luke relaxed in increments—one shoulder drop at a time—until he was almost smiling. Almost laughing.

I caught myself watching him too long.

"You okay?" he asked, leaning toward me, voice low. He smelled like citrus and pine and some kind of soap that made me want to bury my nose in his shirt.

I nodded. "I'm just…glad you came."

Something flickered in his eyes. Something vulnerable.

"You make it easier," he said quietly, squeezing my hand under the table and making sparks shoot up my arm.

Before I could answer, a guy appeared at the edge of the booth—mid-30s, hair gelled within an inch of its life, holding two IPAs.

"Hey," he said to me, "sorry to interrupt, but are you with them or...?"

Luke stiffened beside me.

"I'm with them," I said, smiling politely.

"Because if you're not, I'd love to buy you a drink."

Luke's hand dropped to my knee under the table.

The guy clocked it and backed off with a muttered apology. I turned toward Luke slowly.

His expression didn't waver, but his thumb was moving gently across the inside of my knee in a slow, absent circle.

"You okay?" I asked.

He looked at me. "Do you want me to let go?"

No. I absolutely did not.

But I didn't say that. I just shook my head.

He didn't move his hand.

BY THE TIME the band launched into another set, Luke and I were sitting so close, we were practically sharing a space. His knee pressed to mine. His voice was low and steady in my ear.

"You're different here," I whispered at one point.

He arched a brow. "How so?"

"Quieter. Observing."

"People expect a version of me I don't always want to be," he said, sipping his beer. "You're the only person here who doesn't."

I swallowed. "That's not true. They love you."

He didn't answer. Just looked at me for a beat too long.

And I realized I wasn't the only one watching.

Nick elbowed Christopher. Liam raised a brow. The conversation shifted, but the vibe changed—like everyone had picked up on the gravitational pull between us.

Later, as we waited for the valet, Luke leaned against the wall and glanced sideways.

"Thanks for coming out," he said.

I pressed my lips together and nodded. "Thanks for coming with me."

He hesitated, then added, "And for saying no to that guy. I know you didn't have to."

I looked at him. "You didn't let go."

His gaze dropped to my mouth and stayed there a beat too long.

"No," he said. "I didn't."

CHAPTER 18

An hour later — Ellie

We got home at nearly midnight, yet I somehow convinced Luke to watch my favorite rom-com. We were snuggled up in the giant sectional in the basement, but I have to admit I wasn't paying much attention to the movie. I was preoccupied with what had happened tonight.

I hadn't realized how much I missed *being out*—real drinks, real laughter, real clothes that didn't involve elastic waistbands. And yet, all night, it wasn't the music or the drinks or even the hilariously inappropriate tour stories from Nick and Liam that had made the night feel different.

It was Luke.

Luke beside me at the booth, shoulder brushing mine. Luke looking like every magazine spread I'd ever secretly saved to Pinterest and pretended was about "lighting." Luke, who didn't let go of my knee when someone else tried to buy me a drink.

And it wasn't about ownership. It didn't feel like a claim. It felt like…recognition.

Like something he'd been trying not to see finally clicked into focus.

The movie had ended, the credits had rolled, and still… we hadn't moved.

Luke was beside me on the couch, his left arm tucked protectively against his ribs, his right hand draped across the back cushion behind me. I could feel the warmth of him. The solidness.

"I didn't hate that," he said quietly.

"The movie?"

He nodded. "Even though it was pretty much a chick flick."

I turned toward him slowly. "Oh, no! You liked a rom-com. Should I call the tabloids?"

He chuckled. "You should probably call my therapist."

His eyes were dark in the low light. Watching me. Seeing too much.

"Thanks for going out with us tonight," he added.

"You already thanked me," I pointed out. I didn't mention that going out with his friends had been a strategy. In addition to getting him out of the house again, per his therapist's advice, it had helped me too. It had been a way to let someone else distract me from what I was starting to feel too much of.

But I hadn't wanted to leave Luke.

Luke shifted closer. Barely. But I felt it like a ripple across my skin.

"Ellie," he said, voice a little rough.

I looked at him.

And then he kissed me.

Slow. Certain. Like he'd been thinking about it all day and had just now allowed himself to act. His hand cupped the side of my face, thumb brushing just under my cheekbone, and I sank into him without thinking.

He kissed like he was afraid I'd vanish.

I kissed like I already knew I would.

The world narrowed to breath and heat and the hitch in my chest when he pulled back for half a second, looked at me like I was everything, and kissed me again—deeper this time.

His right hand slid to my waist. My fingers curled into his shirt.

"Ellie," he whispered against my mouth, like a question. Like a prayer.

I froze.

It was instinct—something deep and cold and uninvited. My whole body screamed *yes*, but my brain whispered louder: *You're just another girl. One of many. A temporary nurse. A break in the noise.*

I pulled back.

Luke blinked. "What's wrong?"

"I can't," I said, breath catching.

He sat up straighter, searching my face. "Did I hurt you?"

"No. No—it's not that. It's just—" I stood up too fast. "I can't be the girl who sleeps with you and then pretends it doesn't matter."

His brows pulled together. "Ellie—"

"I've seen you on stages. In magazines. But even before that...I knew the kind of women who come and go from your life."

His voice was low, insistent. "You're not one of them."

"You don't know that." Why was it nearly hard to breathe?

He got to his feet, slower, right hand resting on his hip. "I do."

I shook my head. "I can't be...I'm not just some Florence Nightingale fantasy who got a little too close."

Luke flinched. "Is that really what you think?"

"No." I swallowed. "But I don't know how not to think it."

He exhaled sharply, like he wanted to argue—but didn't know where to start.

"I just need a little space," I said, my voice barely above a whisper. "To think. To breathe."

He didn't stop me as I hurried out of the room.

But I felt his eyes on my back the entire time.

CHAPTER 19

Wednesday night — Ellie

I managed to stay away from Luke the entire next day. Well, most of it. Except for the part where I had to *do my job.*

I changed his bandage with complete and utter professionalism. He tried to say something, but I shut it down pretty quick. The minute I left his room, I called Gran. She told me to stop worrying and start living. I told her it was way easier to dole out advice than take it.

She didn't argue.

But after we hung up, her words lingered. Why had I panicked last night? Luke wasn't a stranger. He was a rock star, a flirt, a heartbreaker. What exactly was I expecting? And if he *had* kissed me... Well, that would've made one hell of a memory. The kind you stash away to smile about when you're eighty.

Maybe Gran was right. Maybe I was taking it all way too seriously. Maybe it was time to loosen my grip and just live a little.

Like a good coward, I'd already asked for dinner to be brought up to my room. But I'd eaten and scrolled way too much through my social media accounts.

It was official. I was bored.

But I was also in a mansion, with a game room and a workout room and a…hot tub.

I dug through my drawer until I found the white bikini I'd bought on a whim with Luke's credit card. The straps cut a clean line across my collarbone. I wrapped myself in a plush white towel from the bathroom and padded downstairs, letting the hum of the house fade behind me.

Steam curled from the hot tub, catching the glow of recessed lights. I set my phone on the ledge, tossed my towel over a chair, and slipped in slowly, the heat rising to my shoulders. The jets pulsed, unraveling a tension I hadn't realized was wound so tight.

I tilted my head back, let my eyes close.

And then—

My phone buzzed.

Luke Knightley:

You still up?

I smiled.

Me:

Maybe.

Another buzz, almost immediately.

Luke Knightley:

I'm sorry about…last night.

Me:

No apology needed.

Luke Knightley:

I feel like something is unresolved
between us.

Me:

You might be right.

Luke Knightley:

You just looked so good.

The message stole the breath right from my lungs.
Not pretty. Not nice.
Good.
Like I'd done something to him. Like he was still thinking
about it.
My fingers hovered over the keyboard.
Me:

You weren't so bad yourself.

A pause.
Luke Knightley:

I meant what I said. About you making it
easier.

My chest tightened.
Me:

You make it hard to walk away.

A longer pause.

The bubbles of the hot tub fizzed gently around me. My skin felt too warm and too bare and far too aware of what it would feel like if he were here. If he stepped into the room right now. If he saw me like this—half-drenched, heart in my throat, still tasting his kiss in my memory.

My phone buzzed again.

Luke Knightley:

> Where are you? I want to settle this.
> Apologize properly…in person.

I stared at the message.

And smiled.

CHAPTER 20

Two seconds later — Luke

ouldn't you like to know? had been Ellie's reply. I sent back some question marks and a set of prayer hands but she'd stopped answering. Probably for the best. This was dangerous territory. And I was well aware of it.

Eventually, I gave up pretending I was going to relax with TV in my room and headed for the basement. The hot tub sounded like the best idea I'd had all day.

Only when I opened the door, I stopped cold.

Ellie was already standing in the water, her back to me, bare shoulders slick and glistening, her bikini bottoms white and very, very minimal. My brain stopped working. My feet didn't move. Every logical cell in my body told me to turn around and get the hell out of there. I didn't listen.

She turned, startled. "Luke? Please tell me you didn't see me on a security camera."

"No, er, no," I replied, probably too emphatically. "Sorry— I swear I didn't know you were down here." I should have left it at that. But no. Instead, I heard myself say, "But since I am… Can I join you?"

She blinked, surprised, then cleared her throat and gave a little smile. "Sure. Yeah. Come on in."

I stood frozen a second longer. "Are you sure?"

Her grin turned playful. "Just don't splash me."

Well, that was practically an invitation. I dropped the towel, ditched my sling, and stepped into the water, careful to keep my left shoulder above the surface. I sank into the high bench seat, trying not to stare too hard at Ellie, who quickly sat, mostly submerged—except now I was very aware of how not submerged she could become.

"I forgot to tell you," she said, nose crinkling. "I bought a bikini."

"From what I've seen of it, I have zero complaints."

Her cheeks flushed, but she didn't look away. "How's the shoulder?"

"Fine. Doctor said heat would help the muscles too."

"Smart doctor."

We sat in the bubbles for a few minutes, both pretending the water was the most fascinating thing in the world.

Then she moved across to the seat opposite mine—and rose up out of the water just enough that I nearly forgot how to speak. Her skin gleamed. Her bikini top left almost nothing to the imagination. I tried to focus on her face. But I completely failed.

"You know what might make you feel better?" she asked.

That grin. That voice. It hit like a spark to dry leaves. "What?"

"More tequila."

I blinked. "You want to do tequila shots in a hot tub?"

"I'm trying to lighten the mood. You game or not?"

Oh, I was game. Dangerously so. "There's a bottle in the bar."

"I know." Her eyes glittered. "I saw it when you gave me the tour."

"I'll go get it."

I stood, wrapped my towel around my waist, and booked it into the next room, grabbed the bottle, and returned. "No salt, no limes. Hope that's okay."

She took it from me like a pro. "We'll survive."

Ellie tipped the bottle to her lips, her head tilting back as her body rose out of the water again. The tequila glinted in the light. When she handed it back, my mouth was dry for reasons that had nothing to do with alcohol. I took a swig, the burn grounding me in the moment.

"Okay," I said, wiping my mouth. "Tequila truth time."

She raised a brow. "You first."

I met her eyes. "What really happened with the guy? The fiancé."

She went quiet. Then: "I found a text on his phone. It said something like, 'Can't wait to see you later. In bed.'" She gave a humorless smile. "Real subtle. And with an ending like a bad fortune cookie."

"Shit," I murmured.

"Yeah. We were at a restaurant. I told him to lose my number. Then I walked out."

Damn. That was a brutal story. I wanted to find the guy and rearrange his face. But all I said was, "I'm sorry."

"I'm not," she said softly. "Not anymore. Just tired of carrying it around, you know?" She took another swig and wiped her mouth. "Want more?"

I nodded, and we passed the bottle again.

"Your turn," she said, eyes narrowing. "Tequila truth: why didn't you kiss me that night…at Meg's?"

Oh, damn. It really *was* Tequila Truth Time.

I let the memory hit again. The kitchen. The cards. Meg saying goodbye to another guest at the door. Me saying something teasing. Ellie leaning toward me, lips parted. And me—backing up like a coward and saying something inane.

I looked at her now, stunning, fierce, funny as hell. "Because I'm an idiot," I said finally. "That's it. That's the truth."

Her smile was slow and a little wicked. "Good answer."

And damn if I didn't want to kiss her right then—only this time, I didn't move an inch.

CHAPTER 21

First, I couldn't help but think of how proud of me Gran would be if she could see me right now. I mean, I know Sam Elliott is more her type, but still, the tequila and the hot tub were on point.

Second, I wasn't about to let Luke off the hook. I'd been sitting on this question for nearly ten years. All it took was one hot tub, two tequila shots, and a bikini that he couldn't seem to keep his eyes off of.

"Do you have any idea how it felt to be practically the *only* girl you ever rejected?"

His eyebrows launched skyward. "Wait—what? Ellie." He looked stricken, scrubbing a hand over his face. "No. No, no, no. That is *not* what happened."

I leveled him with a glare. "Then what did happen, Luke? Because from my seat on Meg's kitchen stool, it seemed like you were about to kiss me and then you backed away like I had a cold sore."

He exhaled and reached out with his right hand, gently

tugging one of mine from where it had been crossed over my chest. He laced our fingers underwater, his thumb brushing lightly across my knuckles. Not helping, but also…helping.

"You were drunk. So was I. But even if I hadn't been, I never would've kissed you that night."

"Why?" My voice cracked on the word. "Because I wasn't hot enough? Cool enough? Or just because I was *me?*"

"No." His voice was low, serious. "Because you were the one girl I respected too much to hook up with."

The word *respect* hit me like a punch in the gut.

I pulled my hand from his. "Wow. That's a hell of a thing to say."

"I'm serious," he said, meeting my eyes. "I didn't want to screw things up with you. I've never been great in relationships, Ellie. Two months in, and I would've messed it up. I couldn't do that to you. Or to Meg."

I bit the inside of my cheek. I wanted to be mad. But something in his voice stopped me—like the kid I used to know was still buried somewhere in there, still trying not to mess up the things that mattered.

"So what?" I said, trying to keep my chin from wobbling. "You thought I wanted a lifetime commitment and figured I couldn't handle it when you inevitably flaked out?"

His gaze didn't waver. "I thought *I* couldn't handle hurting you. And if I'd kissed you that night, I don't think I ever would've stopped."

Oh.

Well.

Okay, then.

"So, you *did* want to kiss me that night?"

"Oh, hell yes, I did." His voice was low, rough, sincere.

I burst out laughing. I didn't even mean to—it just came roaring out of me like a release valve had snapped.

"All these years, I thought you didn't want me. That I was,

I don't know, just not your type or something." I snorted. "Turns out it was the opposite. You had too much *respect* for me?"

Luke didn't laugh. He just nodded, steady and sure, like he was still waiting for me to believe him.

"Think about it from my perspective," he said, voice still low. "You were Meg's best friend. I wasn't going to kiss you unless I was damn sure."

I took a breath, letting the words sink in. "I guess I never thought about it that way."

He smiled faintly. "If it helps, I think about that night more than I probably should."

My eyes locked on his. Then, slowly, deliberately, I reached under the water and brushed my fingers against his thigh. Once. Twice.

"So what was that you said earlier?" I asked, voice low. "About being an idiot?"

Luke's gaze dropped straight to my mouth.

He shifted toward me, his strong, uninjured arm sliding behind my back, his voice a husky whisper against my lips. "No more talking."

This time, I didn't run.

This time, I kissed him back.

And *holy hell*.

His mouth was warm and hungry and perfect. My arms looped around his neck, fingers tangling in the damp hair at his nape. He pulled me flush against him, his chest bare and slick and unfairly muscular, and I swear I made a noise that could only be described as a moan. An actual moan.

One minute we were two friends in a hot tub, the next I was straddling him, lost in a kiss that felt like a match had been lit inside me. His hand slid into my hair, then down to cradle my jaw, guiding me deeper. My skin sizzled. My brain short-circuited. There was tongue. There was tequila. There was one strong, warm hand splayed across my lower back, anchoring me in a way that felt like a promise and a threat all at once.

Eventually, the kiss slowed, his lips brushing mine in softer, lazier passes—like he was trying to memorize the feel.

That was when I finally managed to move, slipping off his lap and back to my seat across from him. I was breathless. Blinking. Slightly dazed. Every nerve ending in my body was lit up like a Christmas tree, and I was absolutely, one hundred percent not okay.

My lips tingled. My thighs ached. My entire system was a blinking red warning sign that said: *Danger, danger, we liked that way too much.*

Tequila was trouble.

And Luke Knightley?

He was the kind of trouble you never forget.

CHAPTER 22

The middle of the night — Luke

The house was quiet again.

Ellie's footsteps had long since faded upstairs. Dolly was curled at my feet like an unbothered security blanket. The couch in the game room still smelled like her shampoo—some subtle citrus thing that had sunk into the fabric the same way she'd sunk under my skin.

We'd gotten out of the hot tub and ended up on the sofa. Talking. Just talking. But not because I didn't want to kiss her again. In fact, it was all I could think about it. But I didn't want to scare her off.

I should've let it go.

Should've laughed it off. Should've blamed the tequila or the nostalgia or the way her mouth felt like home and a dare all at once.

Instead, I walked to the studio.

Not the big professional one. The real one—the one in the back corner of the house with scuffed wood floors and old-school amps and a stool that still had a cigarette burn from the last time I tried to be someone I wasn't.

I sat down with the guitar I wasn't supposed to touch.

My injured shoulder throbbed just from the motion of lifting it into my lap. I ignored it. Shifted. Adjusted. Found a way to rest the body against my ribs and used the fingers of my right hand to pick at a string. Just one.

The note rang out.

It wasn't clean. Or pretty. Or anything I could put on an album. But it was mine.

I played it again. Then added a second. A third.

A half-melody started to form—just bones and breath. Minor chords. Quiet intervals. Something that felt like want and regret twisted up in the same key.

I mouthed a line under my breath.

She stopped the world with a whisper / then disappeared upstairs.

Another note. Another lyric.

She left a mark I can't play through / one hand tied behind my back.

God, it was stupid. Raw. Not even a full verse.

But it was the first thing I'd wanted to write in months.

The first thing that felt like truth instead of brand.

I tried to move my left hand to strum and hissed as pain shot up my arm. I let it fall again, useless at my side.

I stared at the neck of the guitar. The unfinished chords. The silence pressing in at the edges.

"I would've kissed you that night," I whispered into the room, as if she could still hear me. "If you'd asked."

Dolly lifted her head. Whined once.

I nodded.

"Yeah. Me too."

CHAPTER 23

Thursday morning — Ellie

For a blissful ten seconds after waking, I was cocooned in periwinkle sheets, warm and content. And then it hit me.

Last night.

Hot tub. Tequila.

The kiss.

Correction: the *make-out session that defied reason, physics, and common sense.* My pulse kicked up just thinking about it.

It had been slow and hot and way too good. So good it made me forget everything I knew about Luke Knightley—which was saying something. Because what I knew was this: Luke didn't do relationships. Luke collected flings like guitar picks. Luke had a parade of women who'd probably murder each other for a signed napkin, let alone a kiss.

So what had I been thinking?

Easy answer: I hadn't been.

I'd gone into that hot tub telling myself it was all just

friendly tequila and steam. That I'd keep it light. Keep it business. Then his mouth touched mine, and suddenly I was playing strip poker with my common sense. I'd convinced myself a kiss wouldn't matter. That it was just living a little.

But it *did* matter. Because that kiss had melted me down to my DNA.

And that meant danger. Real, capital-D, *bad idea in a beautiful package* danger. I didn't care what Gran said. I couldn't do it again. Luke Knightley wasn't my future. He'd made it clear—no strings, no settling down, no long-term anything. Meanwhile, I had string. I *was* string. Warm and steady and trying really damn hard not to fall for someone who'd made a career out of staying emotionally uncommitted.

I needed to shut it down. Hard stop. No more tequila. No more flirting. No more kissing the wrong guy and hoping he might turn into the right one.

We'd made out. It was a mistake.

And this morning, I was going to make sure he knew that too.

Two Hours Later – Luke

When Ellie showed up at my door to change the dressing, I wasn't sure what I expected.

Maybe awkward tension like yesterday. Maybe a joke to deflect. Maybe a look that said, *last night was fun, but let's never speak of it again.* What I wasn't ready for was…nothing.

She walked in like usual—calm, brisk, like she hadn't spent last night in my lap, kissing me like she meant it.

"Knock knock," she said, already halfway into the room.

"Hey." I stood and tried to sound casual. Like my brain hadn't been replaying her mouth on mine since two a.m.

She folded her arms across her chest and fixed me with a steady gaze. "Look…"

Ah. There it was. Nothing good ever followed *look*.

"About last night…" she said, her voice firm. Professional. "I think we can both agree that kissing was a mistake."

She waited for me to nod. So I did. Because what else could I do?

Even if every molecule in my body wanted to disagree.

"Totally," I said, forcing a nod. "Mistake."

Her face shifted—relief, maybe. Or disappointment. I couldn't tell.

But damn, did it sting to agree with her. Especially when all I wanted to do was rewind and kiss her all over again— this time slower. This time even longer.

I shoved my right hand in my pocket and reminded myself of the facts.

Fact: Ellie was Meg's best friend.

Fact: She was kind and grounded and *good*—and I was a guy in therapy for trust issues, post-trauma paranoia, and commitment phobia.

Also fact: Ellie wasn't a casual thing. Not someone I could kiss and forget.

Which meant she was off-limits.

The thing was, I hadn't dated anyone since getting famous. Not really. Not without a PR rep vetting them or a pit in my gut, wondering if they were in it for the right reasons. Mark told me horror stories—fake pregnancies, black mail, women trying to sell tell-alls for six figures. And that was *before* the nurse snuck photos of me half-naked and sold them to the press.

So yeah, the idea of falling for someone? Not just terri- fying—damn near impossible.

But last night, for one steam-filled, starry moment, I'd let myself forget all of that.

And the truth? I wasn't sorry we kissed.

I was only sorry we'd have to pretend it never happened.

CHAPTER 24

Later Thursday morning — Ellie

Meg might've been hundreds of miles away in Milwaukee, but that's what phones and Face-Time were for. I tapped her contact, twisting at my ring finger like I was wringing the guilt out of it. She picked up on the second ring, her face filling my screen.

"Hey, you," she said. "How's life in Chateau Knightley? Did Luke do something stupid already?"

I exhaled. "How's Mrs. Timms?"

"She's out of the hospital. Jeremy wants to stay a few extra days to be sure she's okay."

I nodded. "That's good. Very responsible."

I took a deep breath. I wasn't sure how long I had to wait before I confessed, but thankfully, Meg jumped right in.

"So? How's it going with my disaster of a brother? Arm still attached?"

"Still functioning. So is the rest of him, unfortunately."

She narrowed her eyes. "Please tell me you didn't call just to say you're fighting again."

"No. We're not fighting. But I have to tell you something. First, though, you need to pretend Luke isn't your brother."

Her expression went flat. "Why. What did he do? If he said something awful, hand him the phone. I swear to God—"

"No, no, it's not like that." I took a steadying breath. "Okay. Deep breath, Meg. This is going to come as a huge shock. Are you ready?"

Meg stared. "You're stalling."

"Luke and I kissed." I winced and squeezed my eyes shut, waiting for a dramatic gasp or a scream or—

"I'm not surprised."

My eyes flew open. "Excuse me?"

Meg shrugged. "I mean...you two have had unresolved sexual tension since high school."

My jaw dropped. "That is categorically false."

Meg rolled her eyes so hard I could practically hear them click. "Ellie. You've been throwing sparks at each other since you were fifteen. You just called it loathing. Everyone else called it foreplay."

I clutched my chest like a scandalized church lady at a strip club. "It was *not* foreplay. That's slander."

"Mm-hmm. So what happened? Wine? Full moon? Did he serenade you in the hot tub?"

I groaned. How did she know? "It was tequila, not wine, and it was just a kiss."

Meg smirked. "Uh-huh. You *sure* it was just a kiss?"

"Yes!" I shrieked. "Well—mostly."

Her grin widened. "I'm just saying. I always figured it would happen eventually."

I pointed toward the phone. "Why didn't you *tell* me you thought that?!"

"Because I assumed *you* knew. And honestly? I thought you'd already kissed years ago."

I blinked. "We didn't. And we're not doing it again. It was a moment. A mistake. Tequila. And this stupid house has too many candles and mood lighting and unfairly soft towels."

"Sounds like a rom-com setup."

"Meg."

"I'm just saying… If that kiss felt like a mistake, it was the good kind. You need one of those."

"He's your *brother*!"

"Exactly. And I know him. Luke's not a total lost cause. He's been through hell this year, and he's finally opening up to someone. And that someone is you."

I scowled harder. "Don't start imagining a future here. I'm not falling for Rockabilly."

"Okay." She lifted her hands, the picture of innocence. "But if you're *so sure* it was just a one-time thing…why did you call me?"

I blinked. "Because you're my best friend. And I needed to tell someone before I exploded. Even if that someone has a genetic connection to the kissing party in question."

Meg's grin turned positively wolfish. "Then here's my advice: kiss him again. Because clearly, you both need it."

CHAPTER 25

Thursday night — Ellie

Meg had ended our call with, and I quote, "A little kissing never hurt anyone."

To which I'd replied—on-brand and predictably defensive—"Your brother is a complete player."

"Allegedly *former* player," she'd said. "But who cares? As long as you both know it's not serious, what's the big deal? You're grown-ass adults. Kiss him. You don't have to marry him."

And damn it, she made sense. I was acting like I had to either slap Luke's hand away or start drafting wedding vows. There was no middle ground in my brain. Just doom or forever.

But now, a few hours later, the clouds of irrational panic had lifted. I could make out with Luke and not spiral into a romance-novel meltdown. It was fine. I was fine. I was a grown-ass adult. Meg said so.

Armed with that questionably empowering thought, I marched downstairs for dinner, mentally prepared for fajitas, per an earlier conversation with Linda, and, if the opportunity presented itself, a little more kissing. Strictly recreational. You know? Like yoga. Or rollerblading.

Luke was already in the kitchen, snacking on guacamole and tortilla chips. The smell of roasted veggies and sizzling meat filled the air. Dolly wagged her entire butt when she saw me.

"Smells amazing," I said brightly, petting Dolly.

Luke looked up, chip halfway to his mouth. "Don't worry. The tequila's still downstairs," he said. "And I have no intention of getting it."

First test of the night. Time to channel Gran and sass it up. "I wouldn't mind. Last night was kinda fun."

Two seconds later – Luke

WAIT. What?

Was Ellie…*flirting?*

This was the same woman who, hours ago, declared our hot tub make-out session a mistake with the solemnity of a Supreme Court ruling. Now she was tossing around casual banter and looking way too good in tight jeans and a green sweater that made her eyes practically glow?

I blinked, trying to recalibrate. "I can get you some wine," I said, as if I hadn't just had a brain short-circuit.

"Sounds good."

I grabbed my phone and made a beeline for the wine room. Ostensibly, I was retrieving her favorite pinot. In reality, I was hiding in the pantry and panic-calling my sister.

She picked up with a cheerful, "Hey."

"It's me," I whispered.

"No kidding. I have caller ID."

"I need your advice."

"Why are you whispering?"

"Because I'm currently hiding next to a bottle of cabernet, and I don't have time to explain. Did Ellie say anything?"

"About what?"

Oh, Meg was enjoying this.

"You know *what*. The kiss."

"She told me."

I scrubbed a hand through my hair. "And?"

Meg paused, clearly savoring the moment. "And I told her: who cares? A little kissing never hurt anyone."

I blinked. "You told her that?"

"Sure did."

I shook my head. "What did she say?"

"She said a lot of things. But I'm not violating bestie code. I *will* say this: you two need to chill out. You kissed. You're both single. Big whup. Kiss her again or don't, but stop acting like someone's going to call HR."

The line went dead. I stared at my phone.

No big deal? That was Meg's advice?

I tucked the phone away and scrubbed my hand through my hair again. Maybe she was right. Maybe Ellie was acting flirty tonight because she'd decided it wasn't a big deal. And if the choice was *kiss her again or don't…*

I knew exactly which side I was on.

Besides, the tequila had already cracked the door open. No use pretending Pandora's box hadn't been flung wide.

CHAPTER 26

Even later Thursday night — Ellie

Somehow, Luke and I ended up on the couch again. This time, he sat a little closer. Not close enough to be obvious, but enough that my entire body was aware of him. And sure, I'd told him the kiss was a mistake, but after my chat with Meg, I wasn't so sure I believed that anymore. I definitely didn't *feel* like it was a mistake. Which was probably why I casually scooted a little closer and finished my wine for courage.

Meg was right. We were adults. Responsible, emotionally intelligent, tequila-free adults. What was a little kissing, really? It was childish to make a big deal out of it.

"The guys are coming over tomorrow for a session," Luke said, rubbing his hand over his forehead. He looked… nervous. Luke Knightley—human embodiment of swagger— nervous. It was oddly endearing.

"Your bandmates?" I asked, trying not to stare at his mouth.

"Yeah. We're gonna…uh…practice."

Definitely nervous. My lips curved. Was *I* making *him* nervous?

"That'll be tricky, right? With the arm?"

"Yeah. Just vocals for now." He shifted slightly, as if the couch was suddenly less comfortable. I got the sense he wanted to say something else but wasn't sure how.

My phone buzzed in my back pocket. I pulled it out, shielding the screen just in case.

Meg:

> Luke called me earlier to ask about you.
> Pretty sure he wants to kiss you again. Want
> me to ask if he's free for prom?

My jaw dropped. *He called her?* I tapped out a single mind-blown emoji.

Meg responded instantly with something that looked like a prom emoji that shouldn't exist, but apparently does.

Okay. No more texting Meg.

I shoved the phone back in my pocket.

"Everything okay?" Luke asked, his hand sliding along the back of his neck.

"Yep," I said far too brightly, bobbing my head like I was on a job interview for a role I had no qualifications for.

"You want to watch TV?"

Sure. Let's pretend we're just two friends. Two friends with unresolved sexual tension so thick it could be cut with a tortilla chip.

"Sure," I said, with more nodding.

Luke glanced down at the couch cushions. "Uh oh. I think the remote fell down in there somewhere."

The remote was, naturally, on the side of his sling. And he looked about ready to stand and retrieve it with his uninjured arm, but I held up a hand. "I got it."

I leaned across him, plunging my hand between the cushions. Unfortunately, the couch was approximately the size of a king mattress and my arm was not. I kept going, leaning farther, hair brushing his thighs, torso halfway across his lap, face now alarmingly close to—

Oh. Oh no. That wasn't a wrinkle in his jeans.

I froze.

He made a low sound in his throat. A groan. Which did *nothing* to help the situation.

I tried to backtrack, but Luke's hand came to my shoulder, firm and warm.

"Ellie," he said, voice low, rough.

The next thing I knew, his lips found mine like they'd been looking for me all day. And maybe they had.

Our mouths collided with the kind of intensity that made thinking completely irrelevant. One thigh slid over his. My hands dove into his hair. He groaned again when my hips shifted. I accidentally nudged his sling. "Ouch."

I pulled back. "Sorry—"

He hauled me closer with his right hand and crushed our mouths back together, effectively ending the apology.

"I didn't really want to watch TV," I whispered.

"Neither did I," he said against my lips.

His hand skimmed up my side, fingers curving around the back of my neck as he deepened the kiss. I let myself melt into him, into this, tasting salt and heat and something wild. When his tongue slid against mine, I moaned—actual, involuntary, full-body-shiver moan.

His mouth left mine to travel a delicious path down my jaw to my ear, where he nipped gently, sending sparks down my spine. I arched against him. He shifted beneath me. We were a tangle of limbs, hot breath, and wanting.

He found the hollow of my neck and kissed it like it was something sacred, and I let my head fall back to give him more. My fingers roamed—shoulders, chest, abs. Good God, the man was built. My thighs tightened around him and his hand gripped my waist, pressing me firmly against the proof that he was just as affected.

I whimpered. Actually whimpered. And when he angled his mouth back up to mine, the next kiss felt like a promise. Of what, I didn't know. I wasn't sure I wanted to know. I just wanted *more*.

Eventually, I pulled back, breathing hard, lips kiss-swollen, brain pure mush. Luke leaned his forehead against mine, both of us panting.

Well. Damn.

That had been some kissing.

And now I was officially in deep.

CHAPTER 27

I clicked the button to end my video session with Dr. H, then slumped back in my chair, dragging a hand through my hair.

"You're making solid progress," she'd said. "Lunch out was a big step. Not to mention the bar."

I hadn't told her about the kissing. Any of the kissing. That felt…off-limits. How was I supposed to explain making out with the woman hired to take care of me like we were two hormonal teenagers behind the bleachers?

So when she'd asked—very pointedly—"Is this someone you're romantically interested in?" I'd blurted, "No, no, no," in the unconvincing voice of a guy who was definitely lying to his therapist.

To change the subject, I'd asked what she thought my next step should be.

Her answer? "Travel."

I'd blinked. "Like, leave town?"

"Yes. Stay somewhere else for a night or two. Take a trip. Try to enjoy yourself."

She made it sound so simple, like I could just casually grab a bag and stroll through an airport without thinking every person was armed with a camera phone and ill intent.

I told her I had a condo in Miami I'd barely used. She said, "Perfect. Go."

Sure. Perfect. Except for the part where I was already stress-sweating just thinking about it.

Still, her advice did have one upside: it kept my brain distracted from last night. Or tried to.

Because, holy hell, the *kissing*.

Multiple, tequila-free, earth-shattering kisses with Ellie Hoffman. And not just any kind of kisses—the kind that took up permanent residence in your bloodstream. The kind you felt the next morning in your bones.

She'd leaned over me to get the remote and brushed against me in just the right way, and that was it. I was gone. And I'd never been so glad to have a couch swallow a remote in my entire life.

Now, all morning, I'd been pacing, grinning like a fool, glancing at the clock, waiting for her to knock.

When she did, I nearly tripped over myself getting to the door.

"You decent?" she asked, poking her head in.

"Unfortunately," I said with a grin.

She walked in wearing a soft pink sweater and gray leggings that had no business looking that good. I followed her into the bathroom like a man under a spell. She was quieter than usual while changing my bandage, but she wasn't rushing. Her fingers lingered, just enough to drive me insane. Then one hand curved around my shoulder while the other toyed with a belt loop on my jeans.

I snapped.

I pulled her toward me and kissed her hard.

She didn't hesitate. Her arms slid around me—one over my uninjured shoulder, the other low around my waist—and we sank into each other like we'd been waiting all morning for this.

When we finally pulled apart, our foreheads touching, I whispered, "We should probably stay away from the bed."

"Good plan," she breathed, nodding, though she didn't sound too convinced.

I kissed her again. Couldn't help it.

But then her palm flattened against my chest. "Okay. While we're…setting boundaries," she said, catching her breath, "I think we should agree on a few things."

"Like what?" I murmured, already leaning back in.

Her hand didn't move. "Like…this ends when I go back to Milwaukee. No expectations. No strings."

I frowned. "What does that even matter right now?" I was already trailing kisses down her neck, knowing full well what it did to her.

"I'm serious, Luke," she said on a moan. That moan undid me.

"I'm looking for the future Mr. Hoffman," she added. "And this—this is just fun."

I hated that. The whole idea of her future Mr. Whoever made something primal in me flare up.

So I did the only logical thing: I kissed her again. Thoroughly.

She let me. Then helped me hoist her up onto the bathroom counter, wrapping her legs around me as my hand gripped her ass and my mouth found her neck. She tasted like cherries and trouble.

"And…" She pushed my uninjured shoulder until I stepped back. "We should stick to only kissing."

Damn. Why did that sound hotter than it had any right to?

"Fine," I agreed because frankly I would have agreed to anything she asked at that moment.

When my tongue flicked against the shell of her ear, she shuddered against me. I didn't think it was possible to want someone this much without combusting.

Eventually, she pulled back, breathless. "I have to go. I've got a call with the hospital's event coordinator."

"Yeah. I have to meet the guys in the studio," I said, even as I stole one more kiss. Then another. And another.

"You're going to make me late," she whispered, still clinging to me.

"You say that like it's a bad thing."

She giggled and slid off the counter. "I'll see you later, Luke." She winked as she walked out, her long hair flipping over her shoulder like a mic drop.

I stood there, right hand braced on the counter, exhaling hard.

I already wanted to kiss her again.

Yep. I was absolutely, irreversibly screwed.

CHAPTER 28

I called Gran first, timing it perfectly so she'd be at bingo and I could leave a message. I wasn't up for recapping all the recent developments—especially the kissing. I left her a cheerful update about the house, assured her I was eating well, and promised to call back soon with more details. Eventually.

Then I called Mary, the hospital's event coordinator. After I wrapped that call—everything for the gala was still running smoothly without me, thank goodness—I logged on for my weekly chat with Mindy.

Despite her cancer diagnosis, Mindy was more upbeat than anyone I knew. She had a colorful boho scarf wrapped around her head, a bowl of popcorn in her lap, and a sparkle in her eyes that refused to dim, no matter what life threw at her.

Technically, I was supposed to be her mentor. A cheerful adult to help distract her from the worst parts of leukemia treatment. But the truth? She distracted me. Mindy always managed to make me laugh, and she kept me updated on the hospital's Oncology Unit drama like it was a full-blown soap opera. Which, according to her, it basically was. Today's episode included a heated Uno tournament, a love triangle over a goldfish, and a nurse who allegedly broke the vending machine. Gripping stuff.

Talking to her always reminded me what actually mattered. Not obsessing over kisses that had no future. Or guys with rock-star smiles and hands that could undo my resolve with one touch. Okay, well. Maybe I wasn't going to *forget* the kisses. But I could definitely file them under "fun-but-over" as soon as I got back to reality.

"So…" Mindy narrowed her eyes at the camera. "You're hanging out with *Luke Knightley,* aren't you?"

I froze. Crap. She'd figured it out. I never should have underestimated a teen with internet access. "Um. Yep. But *please* keep that to yourself."

"Oh, my God. Like, *the* Luke Knightley?" she asked, eyebrows practically flying off her face. "Lead singer of Whiskey Smoke? Blue eyes. Dark hair? Stupid hot?"

I winced. "You know him?"

"I know of him. And *he is soooo cute,*" she said, waggling her brows with all the enthusiasm of a teen with a celebrity crush.

Double crap. "Yeah, well, we've been friends since forever, so I sort of forget he's famous."

Okay, that sounded grossly name-droppy, even to me. As if I had a pocketful of famous friends and wasn't currently having an ongoing mental spiral about one of them kissing me like it was his damn job.

"What's his house like?" she asked, tossing a handful of popcorn into her mouth.

"Ridiculous. I'll send you a link. There was an article with photos—I mean, purely for real estate purposes."

Mindy smirked like she wasn't buying it.

"Does he have a girlfriend?"

My stomach did a weird little dip. "I…don't think so?" I paused. "I mean, no one's mentioned one." I hadn't exactly asked, but you'd think that kind of detail would've come up somewhere between make-out sessions.

Mindy practically squealed. "Wouldn't it be amazing if you and Luke Knightley started dating?"

Abort. Abort.

"Nope. Not gonna happen." I gave my laptop camera my best dead-serious stare.

Mindy tilted her head. "Why not? You're both single. It makes perfect sense!"

"Still nope," I said, louder this time. I wasn't about to explain Luke's romantic resume to a teenager fighting cancer. The girl deserved *hope*, not a rundown of Luke's dating history.

"You're no fun," she pouted.

"His bandmates are downstairs right now," I offered, attempting a distraction. "They're single…and hot."

"AHEM."

I jumped and looked toward the door—where Luke stood, arms crossed, eyebrow arched, looking like he'd walked into the exact wrong sentence. Crap. Had he heard that?

Oh yeah. Judging by the amused look on his face? He'd definitely heard.

"Uh—hold on, Mindy," I said quickly, muting her.

Luke rocked back on his heels. "Did I just get demoted to 'not the hot single one'?"

I gave him an innocent blink that fooled no one. "I was just…doing community outreach."

He grinned. "Wanted to see if you'd come down to the studio for a bit. Say hello to the guys, hang out."

"Sounds great." My smile was far too big. Honestly, I wanted the earth to crack open and swallow me whole. Or at the very least, a couch cushion with a trapdoor.

"No rush. We'll be there a while."

He disappeared down the hall, and I unmuted Mindy so I could hear her again.

"I'm back."

"Ellie. I just googled them. They are *so hot*." She pointed at me through the screen. "But more importantly, *he* just invited you to hang out with all of them. You better go. Immediately."

I laughed. "Sorry I didn't ask if you wanted to meet him."

"Are you kidding? I want to meet *all* of them. But you should probably tell Luke I know you're there before I show up in the Zoom lobby wearing merch."

Solid point.

"Well, have a good week."

"I *will*. Now *go*. I want details next time."

"Text me if you need anything this week."

She rolled her eyes. "You're worse than Nurse Joan when she lingers during *Bluey* hour with the little kids. Go."

"In her defense, *Bluey* is a really good show. I mean that Hotel episode where Bingo insists on being a 'crazy pillow.' It's—"

"Go!"

"Okay, okay, I'm going." I lowered the screen.

"Oh, wait, Ellie?"

I popped it back open. "Yeah?"

Mindy smirked. "I could see you with Luke or Liam Dashwood. I'll let you decide which one's hotter."

I groaned. "Uh, thanks? But I'm not looking for trouble."

"Sure you are," she replied.

I was smiling as I closed the laptop. And thinking—maybe a little trouble wasn't the *worst* thing in the world.

Fifteen minutes later — Luke

When Ellie peeked into the recording studio, I stopped singing mid-verse. All three of the guys turned to look, and she froze like a deer in headlights.

"Sorry," she whispered, biting her lip. Her cheeks flushed bright pink. She smiled, but I could tell she was nervous—tugging on her ring finger like usual. I'd started to recognize that tic.

And just like that, I wanted to kiss her again.

"It's fine," I said, waving her in with my right hand. "Come on in."

As she turned to close the door, I caught all three of my bandmates staring at me with wide eyes, mouthing, *Still hot.* Yeah. No kidding, geniuses. I've got eyes too.

"Ellie, you remember the guys," I said, nodding toward the idiots.

She gave a little finger wave. "Sure. Hi. Thanks for letting me listen in today."

"Surviving your time with Mr. Personality here?" Holt said from behind the drums.

"If you get bored, just say the word, and I'll take you out," Dashwood offered, grinning like a jackass. Of course he asked her out. That was Liam for you.

"So far, so good," Ellie replied, still fidgeting with her ring finger.

"You're Meg's best friend, aren't you?" Wentworth asked.

"Oh, yeah," Dashwood nodded. "Meg told us her best friend was a nurse practitioner. It all makes sense now."

Ellie's gaze snapped to Wentworth. "Wait—Christopher Wentworth? You used to date Ariana Remington, Jeremy's sister, didn't you?"

Wentworth went stiff. Shit. No way Ellie could've known that was a landmine. The Ariana saga was strictly off-limits, unless Wentworth was drunk enough to overshare, which thankfully, he wasn't.

"Uh. Yeah," he mumbled, staring at his guitar like it had suddenly become complicated.

Ellie, to my relief, pivoted. "So how did you all meet anyway?"

"We were in San Francisco," Dashwood said, jerking a thumb at me. "This guy used to come watch my old band. One night after a set, he bought me a beer and told me I was too good for them."

Ellie looked at me, surprised. "You said that?"

I shrugged. "Wasn't wrong."

"It took him a while to convince me to move to Milwaukee," Dashwood said, clearly proud of the story. "But damn glad I did."

Dashwood gave Ellie a grin I'd seen melt entire crowds. I nearly rolled my eyes.

"And I joined after they came back to Milwaukee," Holt added, thankfully steering the attention off Dashwood.

"And Wentworth and I have known each other since high school, of course," I added.

"You all make a great team," Ellie said warmly. "Your success has been amazing."

"It's all Knightley," Dashwood replied. "He wouldn't let us quit."

Her gaze swung to me. "You were going to quit?"

"We thought about it," Dashwood said with a shrug. "First year was pretty rough."

Ellie gave me a smile that made something catch in my chest. "Well, I think it's amazing. I'm glad you stuck with it."

I suddenly felt a little taller. Hell. She thought I was *amazing?*

"So…I can stay for rehearsal?" she asked next.

"Sure. You can sit next to me," Dashwood offered. *Winked.* Jesus. That was fast.

Before she could reply, I nudged out the stool beside me with my foot. "I saved you a spot, Ell."

Yeah. I'd never called her that before. But now seemed like the time to start. Dashwood could back the hell off.

Ellie hesitated for just a beat before smiling and walking over. "Thanks."

I resisted the urge to brush her hair behind her ear. She still smelled good. Distractingly good. Warm vanilla. I needed to focus.

"Wanna hear our new song?" I asked.

"I'd love to."

Wentworth started the bass line, and I closed my eyes and sang. I couldn't play guitar with my arm in a sling, but I could still do what mattered.

When I opened my eyes again, Ellie was swaying gently to the rhythm, her lips curved in a soft smile. Watching her like that—looking proud of us, proud of *me*—did something to my chest.

We played two more songs while Ellie sat beside me, relaxed, tapping her fingers on her thigh. When we wrapped, she clapped. "That was fantastic."

"You really liked it?" Dashwood jumped in before I could.

I clenched my jaw. *I* was going to ask that.

"Yeah, I really did," Ellie said, eyes on me now. Her smile grew.

Damn. That smile.

As the guys packed up, Ellie looked around. "So none of you were hurt in the accident?"

"I wasn't on the bus," Dashwood said, smirking.

"Yeah, he was with a groupie," Wentworth muttered.

"She was a *fan*," Dashwood replied with mock offense.

Ellie smirked. "Sounds like you got lucky in more ways than one."

The guys cracked up. Okay, Ellie was *funny* too.

"I just had a couple scratches," Wentworth said, reeling it back in. "Same with Nick. Mark and the driver were fine."

"Glad to hear it," she replied.

"So, Ellie… You never said the other night. Are you single?" Dashwood was grinning from ear to ear.

I snapped. *"Dash,"* I growled.

"What?" he asked, hands raised like he was innocent. Please.

"Don't hit on Meg's best friend," I barked. "She's not here for your bullshit."

Dashwood's eyes gleamed. "You mean your *nurse* isn't here to be sexually harassed? Or that you've got a thing for her, and you're mad I noticed?"

He wasn't wrong. But I didn't say a word. I just glared.

And from the way Ellie ducked her head and smiled into her lap, I wasn't the only one who liked the idea.

CHAPTER 30

Friday night — Ellie

I dressed up a little more than usual for dinner. Nothing dramatic—just a black mini skirt, a puff-sleeved sweater, my go-to pink gloss, and a pair of gold hoops. But I wasn't fooling myself. I'd dressed for Luke.

The image of him singing earlier was still playing in my head like a music video I couldn't turn off. Watching him that close—his voice all gravel and smoke, his Adam's apple working as he sang with his eyes closed—I'd nearly fanned myself. That voice should come with a warning label. Honestly, if I'd been alone, I might've made an embarrassing noise. But I'd kept it together. Barely.

I remembered being fourteen and watching him play guitar on the porch at the trailer park.

It had been a warm summer night, fireflies blinking in the grass, and Luke sitting on the stoop with his head tilted down, calloused fingers moving over the strings like it was the only thing in the world. I'd hidden behind my screen door, just listening. Watching.

He looked untouchable then—reckless and radiant in a way that made my chest ache. I told myself it was just admiration. A passing thing. But even now, I remembered the exact shape of that ache.

And the way I'd shoved it down so fast, it practically left a bruise.

That was the first time I told myself Luke Knightley was not an option.

Apparently, that memo hadn't made it to my hormones.

Speaking of hormones. Mindy hadn't lied. Luke's bandmates were also hot. Seeing them in the brighter lights in the studio today had confirmed it. Liam had that whole charming-bad-boy thing, Christopher was quietly intense, and Nick looked like a Calvin Klein ad behind the drums. But I wasn't paying much attention to them—not really. Because Luke had gone all possessive when Liam started flirting, and that had been…something. It wasn't that he was *jealous*—I mean, players didn't get jealous—but it had definitely read a little…territorial.

Which, I won't lie, was hot.

By the time I made it to the kitchen, Dolly was waiting at the door like she'd missed me all day. I crouched to rub her head. "Did you have a good day, sweet girl?"

"She did," came a low voice behind me.

Luke emerged from the pantry holding a bottle of my favorite pinot noir. His hair was still damp and pushed back, and he was wearing jeans and a pale blue button-down—paired with his ever-stylish navy sling. And yeah. He looked stupid hot.

"Hope you're in the mood for comfort food," he said, setting the bottle down. "Linda made grilled chicken, mashed potatoes, and green beans. With salad."

"Sounds perfect," I said, ignoring how my stomach flipped at how *domestic* it felt.

He poured my wine without asking, which felt way too couple-y. Not that I minded. But still. I took the glass and tried to focus on literally anything except how much I wanted to kiss him again.

"So, Meg texted," I said. "She and Jeremy are coming back tomorrow morning."

"Yeah. She told me. Sounds like Mrs. Timms is doing better."

"Good news." Great, now I was doing that awkward head-bob thing again.

Because all I could think about was when we could get back to the kissing.

Luke took a sip of his beer, eyeing me over the rim of the glass. "What'd you think of rehearsal?"

"Loved it." I sipped my wine, then added innocently, "Remind me—who's single again?"

His eyes narrowed. "Why? You taking notes?"

"Just curious," I said, fluttering my lashes. "Liam seemed nice."

Luke muttered something under his breath, then said, "He's not."

"Oh?" I raised an eyebrow.

"He's not dangerous or anything," Luke clarified. "Just... not exactly known for long-term commitments."

I sipped again, hiding my grin. "Huh. That sounds familiar."

Luke's eyes narrowed further. "I'm *not* like Dashwood."

I set my glass down. "No? Because your dating history doesn't exactly scream commitment either."

"I've never lied to anyone. Never promised anything I didn't mean." He paused, then added, "But yeah, I've been an idiot. That's fair."

I blinked. Honestly? That was new.

"I just…" he continued, rubbing the back of his neck. "I didn't like the way he looked at you."

My heart thumped. "No?" I tried to sound casual.

"No." He stepped closer, his voice dropping. "Truth? I wanted to punch him."

That earned him a smile. "That's very caveman of you."

He didn't answer. Just closed the distance, slid an arm around my waist, and buried his face in my neck. I gasped.

Then his mouth moved to mine—slow, deep, addictive. And when he whispered, *"I don't want anyone touching you but me,"* against my ear, I nearly melted into the hardwood.

Hot. Damn.

Somewhere in the haze of tongue and lips and his hand sliding to the small of my back, we made our way to the couch, completely abandoning dinner. Priorities.

And when I say the kissing was hot? I mean *hot.* Better than sex I'd had in the past. I was ruined. Absolutely ruined.

And still somehow pretending it didn't mean anything.

We'd agreed. It was just kissing.

Just two grown adults…kissing like they couldn't breathe without each other.

No big deal. Right?

Right.

Maybe.

Probably not.

CHAPTER 31

Meg and Remington returned just before dinner, and if I could've magically teleported them back to Milwaukee, I would've done it without an ounce of guilt. Especially with the way Ellie kept sneaking glances at me—hot ones. The kind that made it impossible to focus on anything but the fact that I hadn't kissed her in hours.

And judging by the heat in her eyes when Meg wasn't looking, she wanted to kiss me just as badly. But neither of us was about to start pawing each other in front of her best friend and my sister. There were still lines. Faint ones, maybe. But they existed.

Barely.

By the time we finally made it to the game room and played a few rounds of darts—which I completely sucked at, thanks to being one-armed—I was barely hanging on. And when Meg and Remington called it a night and the door clicked shut behind them, I didn't waste a second.

I crossed the room, slid my arm around Ellie's waist, and murmured, "I thought they'd *never* leave."

Her smile was wicked. "Me too," she said—just before I kissed her.

Hard.

Her mouth opened against mine and I pressed closer, my hand slipping around her back as I inhaled her perfume and nuzzled my face into her neck. I kissed her there—once, twice—then trailed my lips along her collarbone until she shivered.

"Come on," I whispered, my voice low and rough.

I pulled her with me to the loveseat and we sank into the cushions, bodies turned toward each other, thighs pressed together. My hand drifted to her leg, just high enough to make her eyes spark. She didn't move away. Didn't say a word. Just gave me that sly grin that killed me every damn time.

I surprised us both by not diving in for another round of kissing. Instead, I said, "So…my therapist wants me to take a trip."

"A trip?" She blinked. "Like…a *trip* trip?"

"Yeah. Like leave-the-house-for-a-couple-of-nights kind of trip." My hand stayed on her thigh. "She thinks I need to prove to myself that I can still enjoy things outside these four walls and this city."

Ellie leaned her head on my shoulder. The move was casual. Easy. But it felt like…more.

"I mean," she said, "that sounds healthy and good and all, but also… Does this mean the kissing goes on pause while you're gone?" She grinned up at me. Teasing. But not really.

I laughed. "That's the problem. I don't really want to go without you."

Her smile faltered for just a second before her fingers started tracing circles on my jeans. Torture.

"So don't," she whispered.

I shifted to face her fully and took her hand. "Come with me."

That did it. Her head snapped up, and she immediately started coughing.

"Whoa—okay, didn't mean to be a choking hazard," I said with a soft laugh.

She waved her hand, eyes watering. "You want me to go with you…on a trip?"

I nodded, suddenly way more nervous than I should've been. "I feel better when you're around, Ellie. And I know it's not part of the job description, but this isn't about that. It's about me not turning into a hermit."

Of course, it was more than that. I wanted to see where this thing between us might lead. But she'd made me promise —just a fling, nothing lasting. Everything would go back to normal when she went back to Milwaukee. I couldn't imagine that now, but I kept the thought to myself.

She stared at me for a beat. Then two. "Where were you thinking?"

I bit my lip. "I was thinking…Miami."

Her eyes widened. "Miami?"

"Yeah. I've got a place there. Haven't used it much. I figured it's a good place to ease back into the world."

She blinked. "I've never been to Miami."

I gave her a slow smile. "Wanna try it with me?"

Her lips curved up. "Only if you promise not to challenge me to darts again. It was a little sad."

"Deal," I said, leaning in close. "But just so you know, I'm way better at strip poker."

Her cheeks flushed, but she didn't look away. "Miami, huh?"

"Think about it."

"Oh, I will," she said, voice low. "Believe me—I will."

CHAPTER 32

Two seconds later — Ellie

Every rational part of my brain was throwing red flags like confetti. I *shouldn't* want to go to Miami with Luke. But I did. And that scared the hell out of me.

I needed to pause and do a mental sort. Did I want to go because I was technically still his nurse and this was part of supporting his therapy? Or because the idea of him being far away—and me not being there to kiss him senseless—felt like a loss I wasn't ready to take?

Maybe it was both.

Maybe it was neither.

Maybe I was already too far gone.

Because let's be real: I *would* miss the kissing. The way he used his mouth on my neck made me want to melt into the floor and hand him the keys to every last piece of clothing I owned. I hadn't done it yet—but not for lack of fantasizing. Repeatedly. In detail.

And then he'd gone and surprised me. One second, we

were making out on the loveseat. The next, he was talking about taking a trip together, and I'd barely caught up in time to hear him ask me to come with him. His voice had gone all soft and uncertain, like the Luke I remembered from years ago—before the fame, the fans, the chaos. It was disarming. Sweet. And yeah, heart-squeezing.

Also—sidebar—he owned a place in *Miami*? And that somehow wasn't public knowledge? How had the gossip blogs missed that? Note to self: deep-dive internet search later.

But I didn't have time for Zillow sleuthing. Luke was still watching me, waiting for an answer.

"I don't know," I said, honest and slightly panicked, chewing on my bottom lip.

He swallowed and nodded slowly. "Ellie, I don't want you to feel pressured. You've already done more for me than I ever expected. And if this…" He motioned between us. "If the kissing is messing with the lines between us, I get it. I really do. But…I feel safe with you. And I'd love it if you came with me."

Oh no.

No, no, no. That was an *irresistible* speech. It ticked every damn box: sweet, vulnerable, self-aware, respectful. He was giving me an out—while still saying he wanted me there. How was I supposed to say no to that?

I let out a long breath and stretched my arms toward my knees like I was prepping for a yoga pose. "Okay," I said. "I'll go."

His entire face lit up. He reached for my hand, brought it to his mouth, and kissed it like something out of an old Hollywood movie. "Name your terms," he said, eyes dancing.

I grinned. "We don't stop the kissing."

Luke's smile turned downright wolfish. "Deal."

CHAPTER 33

Sunday — Miami — Ellie

Luke's Miami condo was every bit as jaw-dropping as his Nashville mansion. Towering high above the beach in a sleek new high-rise, it was all glass and steel and *"Holy crap, I'm not in Milwaukee anymore."*

When the black town car pulled up to the entrance, I stepped out into the thick, humid air and let the warm ocean breeze hit my face, a sultry welcome. Palm trees lined the sidewalk. Bougainvillea exploded in hot pink. Hibiscus bloomed like they had something to prove. It was like stepping into a postcard.

Inside, the building lobby was straight out of a Bond villain's lair—white marble, chrome, and glass everywhere. Even the elevators looked like futuristic escape pods, and Luke had to show me how they worked. They only went to certain floors, depending on your key fob, which made me feel both very cool and slightly underdressed.

The condo itself? Floor-to-ceiling windows, three bedrooms, three and a half baths, and water views from what felt like every angle. It was minimal and modern, all neutral tones and slick surfaces. In a word, it was perfect.

Luke had handled the flight and the ride like a pro—no stress, no panic, not even a hint of a sweat. I was proud of him. But I didn't mention it. I figured if he wanted to talk about how it felt to be out in the world again, he'd bring it up.

"Why'd you buy this place if you never visit?" I asked, staring out at the turquoise water nearly hypnotized.

He shrugged. "Business manager said real estate was smart."

"So it's just this and Nashville?" I asked, doing my best *not* to sound like I was cataloging his assets for future-wife purposes. "Or do you also have a secret ski lodge in Aspen and a pied-à-terre in Paris?"

He laughed. "I also have a house on a lake in Green Bay."

"Green Bay?" I blinked. "Seriously?"

He pointed a thumb at himself. "Die-hard Packers fan."

Oh yeah. That tracked. I had a hazy memory of him splayed out on Meg's couch in a green and yellow T-shirt, probably being sarcastic. These days, it was harder to recall the sarcasm. Mostly because every time I thought about Luke, my brain skipped ahead to his mouth on mine. Go figure.

Just then, his phone lit up. He smiled when he saw the screen. "Excuse me a sec," he said, heading toward the bedroom to take the call.

I stayed where I was, trying *very* hard not to wonder who was on the other end or why he'd stepped out. Not my business. Not my place. Instead, I stood at the window and looked out at the water and told myself—again—that this was healthy. Casual. Breezy.

No strings. No expectations. Just kissing.

That had become my mantra ever since I agreed to this

little getaway. I needed to loosen up, have fun, remember that romance didn't have to mean lifelong commitment. It could just mean sun and sand and a few extremely well-placed kisses.

And if anyone had reminded me six months ago that Luke freaking Knightley would be the man to bring my fun side back to life, I would've told them to shut their lying mouth. But here we were.

I called Gran to distract myself, fully expecting to get voicemail. No such luck. She answered on the second ring, breathless and annoyed. "Ellie, I'm in the middle of a mahjong bloodbath. Are you dying?"

"Nope. Just thought I'd check in."

"You're not pregnant, are you?"

"Gran!"

"Well, you sounded weird."

I told her I was in Miami. She told me not to get sunburned or kidnapped (turns out, she'd recently watched a whole *Dateline* about sex trafficking), then she hung up to get back to her tiles. I was still smiling when Luke reappeared.

His phone was gone and that mischievous grin of his was firmly in place. "That was the maître d' at the restaurant I booked for tonight."

"Maître d'?" I arched a brow. "Fancy."

"Very," he said, mock serious, stepping closer and sliding his uninjured arm around my waist. His lips brushed my ear. "Also, I can't wait to get this sling off. I want to be able to wrap both arms around you."

I almost spontaneously combusted.

I had a brief thought that when his sling came off, I'd be on my way back to Milwaukee, and there would be no more kissing, with or without both arms. But I let it go when he kissed me—deep, slow, sinfully thorough. When we finally broke apart, I was breathless and mildly dizzy.

"How about a trip to the pool?" he asked, like we hadn't just made out like honeymooners on a beach escape.

I exhaled, squeezing my thighs together like it might help to stop the aching. "Sure," I said, trying to sound casual and not like I was seconds from leaping on him. "Perfect Miami activity."

He grinned. "Great. I'll throw on my trunks. You grab your suit. Meet you back here in fifteen?"

"Sounds good," I said, already turning toward the bedroom he'd given me. Like a gentleman, he'd made sure I had my own space. Which was smart. Practical. The responsible thing to do.

Even if part of me wanted to ditch the responsible thing entirely.

As I started walking, I couldn't resist glancing back. And there it was—Luke's very fine ass in those fitted jeans.

"Ellie," he called without turning around.

"Yep," I squeaked, eyes snapping upward. He winked over his shoulder.

So he *had* seen me checking him out. Cool, cool, cool.

"We'll hit the pool, come back up, and then we're going out. Gonna paint the town red."

I laughed. "Sounds like a plan."

Except we weren't just going out, were we?

We were going on a *date*. Or at least what seemed like a date.

And I was dangerously close to liking that idea way too much.

CHAPTER 34

Sunday night — Ellie

Turns out *fancy* didn't quite cover it.

Just like in Nashville, the black SUV pulled around to the back of the restaurant, but this time, there were paparazzi waiting in the alley, shouting Luke's name like we were at a movie premiere instead of just going to dinner.

"How did they know you were here?" I asked as we settled into yet another private dining room.

Luke's jaw was tight. "No idea. My guess? Someone at the condo tipped them off about the car."

I watched him for a second. He was clearly pissed, and not just about being spotted—this ran deeper. The wound from his former nurse's betrayal was still raw, even if he didn't talk about it much.

"I'm fine," I said gently, before he could worry about me. And I meant it. If I could handle a cheating ex and a hospital full of personalities, I could handle a couple of loud guys with cameras.

The ultra-efficient waitress placed our drinks the moment we sat. Luke had texted our order from the car. I sipped my dirty martini and scanned the room—dim lighting, glowing candlelight, and crystal vases filled with fresh white roses.

"Do you just bring white roses with you wherever you go?" I asked, raising an eyebrow.

He smirked. "Only when I'm trying to impress someone."

I didn't let myself read into that. Much.

Tonight, I'd gone for timeless: a little black dress I'd picked up back in Nashville. Luke had offered me his credit card again, and while I'd resisted at first, I eventually caved. The man owned a couch that cost more than my car—I figured he could swing a few hundred bucks for a dress. And truthfully? It felt good to be taken care of for once. I'd spent most of my life as the one doing the caretaking—first for Gran, then for everyone else. I was overdue for a break.

And Luke? He looked like something out of a GQ spread. Fitted gray suit. Crisp white shirt. Black tie. Even his sling matched. Seemed unfair.

"I should send Meg a picture of us," I said, laughing. "She won't believe how well we clean up."

Luke grinned. "I don't know about me, but *you* look amazing."

Heat crawled up my neck. "You don't look so bad yourself."

"It's weird, right?" he added. "That Meg didn't say much when we took off for Miami?"

"She knows we've been making out," I said.

His brows rose. "And she's just…cool with that?"

"I know." I sighed. "Suspicious."

Before he could reply, the chef himself came in, welcomed us, and assured us we wouldn't need menus. I braced myself—and then course after course of the most divine food I'd ever tasted started arriving. Chestnut soup. Goat cheese with pancetta and pears. A beets and white bean salad. Brie-stuffed chicken. Chocolate cheesecake. There was even something called a *mignardise,* which sounded made-up but turned out to be miniature macaroons and tiny sips of heaven disguised as espresso.

Between courses, a server came out and *brushed crumbs off the table.* With a tiny silver tool. Who knew that was a job?

"So," Luke asked casually, "how are you liking Miami?"

"I've officially peaked," I said. "That pool guy who misted me with a bottle? Like I was a delicate orchid? The. Best."

He laughed. "That's the goal."

"And yes, my room is perfect." All white everything. Somehow serene and cozy, not sterile. Very Miami chic.

He leaned in, eyes glinting. "Truth?"

"Hit me."

"I gave you the room farthest from mine on purpose. Figured I'd be less tempted to knock."

A thrill zipped down my spine. Luke Knightley keeping his distance…out of temptation? *Cute.*

"Probably for the best," I said, smiling into my martini.

By the time we left—via a side exit and a different car— Luke looked more relaxed than I'd seen him in days. Back at the condo, I kicked off my heels near the front door.

"Dinner was amazing. Thank you."

"My pleasure," he said, tugging off his shoes.

"And thanks for the dress," I added, glancing down at myself.

He gave me a slow once-over. "You're welcome. And judging by the way you look wearing it, it's some of the best money I've ever spent."

"Better than the bikini?" I whispered, biting my lip.

"No," he growled.

I blushed again. This date—because that's what it was, whether we said the word or not—had been perfect.

"You wanna watch a movie?" he asked.

"Sure," I said, heading for the massive white couch. "What do you want to watch?"

I lowered myself to sit on the couch while Luke brought over a champagne bottle and two glasses that had magically already been set up in the kitchen.

Luke handed me a glass and settled beside me, the soft hum of ocean waves drifted through the open balcony doors. We sat there for a long moment, not touching, not speaking —just looking at the moonlight dancing across the water like it was performing for us.

"This place is insane," I said quietly, staring out at the horizon. "Do you ever get used to all of it?"

He shrugged. "Sometimes. Then I remember what my mom's kitchen looked like growing up, and it all feels ridiculous again."

I glanced at him. "Do you ever miss that? The simplicity?"

Luke took a sip and rested the glass against his knee. "Some days. But mostly, I miss feeling...known. Like people saw me for who I was, not just the version of me that's online."

I nodded, letting that sit for a beat. "That's why you asked me to be your nurse. Because I knew you before the spotlight."

"And you never let me get away with anything," he added, smiling faintly.

"Still don't."

He winked at me. "That's the appeal."

I laughed softly. "You have a weird definition of appealing."

Luke's smile faded into something more serious. "You

make me feel like I can exhale. Like I don't have to perform or fix everything."

That quiet honesty hit me right in the chest. I didn't have a clever comeback for that.

Instead, I swirled the champagne in my glass and whispered, "I don't know if I ever really saw you before. Not like this."

His gaze flicked to mine. "And now?"

"Now I'm trying really hard not to like you too much."

The words came out before I could stop them, and I instantly regretted them—not because they weren't true, but because they felt dangerous. Raw. Too much.

Luke's eyes searched mine, but he didn't smile. Didn't tease.

"I already like you too much," he said simply.

The breath whooshed out of me.

I sat down my glass. "Luke…"

"No pressure," he said, voice low. "I just needed you to know."

It was terrifying. It was thrilling. And when I leaned into him, it was not because the champagne went to my head. It was because I believed him.

Because in that moment, with the sound of the waves and the scent of salt in the air, he felt like the safest thing in the world.

"So, how about that movie?" I asked to try to inject a little bit of light-heartedness back into the moment.

The next thing I knew, he was removing his tie, and I helped ease off his jacket and adjust his sling, my fingers brushing his chest. The moment I looked up into his eyes, I knew.

"It doesn't matter what we pick," he murmured. "We're not really going to watch it."

Heat surged through me.

I dropped onto the couch. He joined me in seconds, his mouth finding mine with that now-familiar, delicious urgency. I straddled him carefully, one knee on either side of his hips, my short little dress riding up. His right hand slipped to the back of my thigh, squeezing, guiding me closer. His arousal pressed against me, and I whimpered into his mouth.

Then, with a sudden boldness, I pulled down the sleeves of my dress to reveal the lacy black bra I'd worn on purpose tonight. No more playing coy.

His eyes darkened. "Ellie…"

He kissed down my chest, his tongue tracing the swell of my breast through the lace. It was almost too much. And not enough.

My body was on fire.

But then he pulled back slightly, resting his forehead against mine. "Damn. I wish…"

He didn't finish the sentence. He didn't need to.

We both knew kissing wasn't going to be enough for much longer.

And we were one last excuse away from breaking every rule we'd set.

CHAPTER 35

Monday morning — Luke

I*'m so screwed.*

The thought looped in my head like a song I couldn't turn off as I sat in the jet, watching Ellie sleep beside me on the flight back to Nashville.

I liked her. Like, *really* liked her. Even told her as much. And that was the problem.

Because I was still me—damaged goods with commitment issues and a reputation for bailing—and she was still Meg's best friend. The same Meg who'd made it abundantly clear over the years that Ellie was looking for something real. A future. A husband. Not some temporary detour with a rock star in a sling.

Whose brilliant idea had it been to keep kissing anyway?

Last night, I would've handed over my other arm just to take her to bed. But we'd made a deal. Just kissing. Nothing more. Casual. Fun. No expectations.

Only that was bullshit.

There was nothing *casual* about the way we'd been kissing last night. Nothing light. Nothing remotely friendly. If I'd had full use of both arms, I would've hoisted her up, wrapped her legs around my waist, and taken her straight to bed without a second thought.

The only thing saving us from full-on disaster was a stupid sling and the last ounce of willpower I had left.

When she'd pulled off the straps of her dress and I'd gotten a glimpse of black lace, I'd actually had to *chant calming thoughts in my head*. That's how far gone I was. It wasn't just lust. Not anymore. And that scared the hell out of me.

Because this thing with Ellie? It was already a tangled mess. And I knew myself well enough to recognize the signs. If we didn't stop, we were headed straight for the part where someone got hurt.

What made it worse was how *good* it had been. Not just the kissing. Being around her. With Ellie, the anxiety about crowds and cameras and not trusting anyone seemed to take a back seat. All I wanted to do was take care of *her*. That feeling? That was new. And I didn't know what to do with it.

I looked at her now, curled up peacefully in the seat beside mine, her lips slightly parted, one hand tucked under her cheek. I leaned in just slightly, lowering my voice to a whisper only she could possibly hear.

"What am I going to do with you?"

Because if we didn't pump the brakes now, we were going to crash. And I didn't want to wreck her just because I couldn't keep my hands—or my feelings—to myself.

The worst part? I already knew what I *should* do. I needed to put space between us. Dial it back. Stop the kissing. That had been the whole point of the deal in the first place—keep it simple, keep it safe.

But this hadn't been safe for a while now.

I dragged my hand down my face and let out a long sigh. Pulling back was going to suck. But it was the right thing to do. I'd be doing Ellie a favor.

And if I just kept repeating that long enough, maybe I'd actually believe it.

CHAPTER 36

Monday night — Ellie

Meg and Jeremy went out for dinner. Luke and I barely touched ours. In what felt like minutes, we were tangled up on the couch again—my hands in his hair, his right arm locked around my waist, our mouths fused like we couldn't get close enough.

I wanted more. Desperately.

I was basically begging him—silently, with my body—to slide off my shirt and kiss every inch of me like he had in Miami. Only this time, I wanted the bra gone too. It wasn't subtle. I wasn't subtle. And at this point, I didn't care.

We'd managed to keep it PG-13 in Florida. Mostly. I had no idea how. But since then, I'd thought about it every hour. Maybe we'd started this off as "just kissing," but that agreement was unraveling fast. We were adults. With hormones. And good intentions had left the building the second his hand slid up my thigh.

I pulled back, heart pounding, and forced the words out

through ragged breath. "This is crazy. We obviously both want this. Do you want to come up to my room?"

I expected him to grin. Say something cocky or needy or just, "Hell yes."

Instead, he said, "No."

Just—*no*.

It hit fast, like a sucker punch. I reeled back, physically and emotionally, sliding off his lap and moving toward the end of the couch.

"No?" I echoed, stunned. "Seriously?"

He looked panicked. "Ellie, I'm sorry—"

I held up a hand and forced myself to sit up straight. "It's fine. No worries." Lies. All lies. My stomach twisted. My cheeks burned. And if he said something about "respecting me," I was going to scream.

"Ellie—"

"Don't." My voice was sharper than I intended. "It's not a big deal." Another lie. A huge, gaping, aching lie.

But Luke kept going. "I told myself on the flight home that we needed to stop this. That it was already too much. But seeing you tonight...I'm weak, Ellie. I'm sorry."

God. That was even worse. He'd been planning to end this all day? And here I'd been mentally scheduling round two.

I glanced at him—and there it was. The same pitiful, puppy-dog look Meg had used when convincing me to take this job. Damn it. This was on me. I *knew* Luke was a player. I *knew* better. And I'd let myself hope anyway.

He tried again. "It's been really great, but—"

My head snapped toward him like a heat-seeking missile. "Oh, hell no. You are not letting me down gently right now. We were just kissing. *Just kissing*, remember? No big deal." My voice shook, and I bolted to my feet before he could see the tears building.

I didn't wait for him to respond. I turned before he could say anything else that might crush me further.

I took the back staircase two steps at a time and locked myself safely in my room.

I flung myself on the bed—teenage-drama style, because apparently that's the headspace I was in—and stared at the ceiling in furious silence.

How had I let this happen?

I'd opened the door, let him in, let him under my skin. All while telling myself it didn't mean anything. Just kissing. Just fun. But I don't *do* casual. I never have. And I knew that. I knew who Luke was—he's *always* been this guy. And I still let it happen.

Because *I* was weak.

No, scratch that—I was tired. Tired of holding it all together. Tired of being the caretaker. Tired of acting like I didn't want something more than gauze and flirting. Luke made me feel something real. And for one stupid second, I thought maybe he felt it too.

But I was wrong. Again.

And I should have known.

I *did* know.

But that didn't stop the heat from rising in my cheeks or the hollow ache blooming in my chest. I'd put myself out there—offered something real, vulnerable—and he'd handed me a thank-you note instead of his heart.

Not cruel. Just careful. Like he didn't want to break anything, so he stepped around it.

I continued to stare up at the ceiling, jaw clenched against the sting in my eyes.

God, I felt *stupid*.

Stupid for thinking he might feel the same. Stupid for letting my guard down. Stupid for thinking kisses meant anything other than kisses.

I peeled myself off the bed and changed out of the clothes I'd picked out like a lovesick teenager. I pulled on an old hoodie, yanked the sleeves over my hands, and crawled into bed—but sleep didn't even try to come. The silence pressed down like a weighted blanket in all the wrong ways.

I grabbed my phone.

No new messages. Just the last one I'd sent Meg earlier that night, a dumb picture of tonight's dinner setup with a caption that said, "Tell me this doesn't look like a date."

I typed a new one.

Me:

I asked him to come up. He said no.

She replied almost instantly.

Meg:

Wait. WHAT?

Me:

He said…it's been really great, but…

Meg:

He's an idiot! Oh, Ellie. I'm so sorry.

Me:

I kinda feel like the idiot atm.

Meg:

You're not. You were brave.

Me:

No. I was hopeful. Which might be worse.

There was a pause before her next reply.
Meg:

Do you want me to come back? I'll tell him
how stupid he is.

Me:

No. Please don't!

Meg:

Got it. Remote support only. Also, I hate him
right now. Just FYI.

Me:

Don't. He wasn't mean. Just…kind. And
distant. Like he was saving me from himself.

Meg:

Maybe he was. But that doesn't make it suck
less.

Me:

It really doesn't.

Meg:

Fwiw I think he'll regret this.

I stared at the screen for a long time.

Me:

> I don't even know if he should. That's the
> worst part. He's probably right.

She didn't reply for a moment. Then:
Meg:

> You were honest. And that's what matters.

The ache in my chest sharpened, then twisted.

I turned off my phone and rolled onto my side, burying my face in the pillow.

I missed him. Already. More than I had any right to.

I clenched my jaw against the tears. Damn it. I'd spent too much money—and time—on therapy to let myself spiral over another charming, unavailable man. Luke was never going to be the guy who stayed. And I wasn't the girl who could pretend that didn't matter.

Fine. No more kissing. No more hoping.

Starting now, this thing between us was over. We were going back to the nurse/patient dynamic, and I'd be damned if I let him know he'd hurt me. I was a professional. I'd signed the paperwork. I'd do my job.

And I'd keep my stupid heart out of it.

From now on, Luke Knightley was strictly business.

The kissing was over. For good.

CHAPTER 37

Tuesday morning — Luke

And the Grammy for *World's Biggest Jackass* goes to… me. Luke Knightley. Damn.

I lay flat on my back, staring at the ceiling like it had answers. Spoiler: it didn't.

I ran a hand over my face and groaned. Last night, I'd marched down to dinner with every intention of keeping my hands—and lips—to myself. I was going to be strong. Mature. Respectful.

Then Ellie walked into the room.

And just like that, every ounce of self-control vanished. One look at her and it was like a damn tractor beam locked on. We didn't even *talk*. One second we were making polite conversation, saying goodbye to Meg and Remington, and the next we were on the couch making out like teenagers in a borrowed basement.

And when she asked me to come to her room? My stomach dropped straight to the floor. Did I want to? Hell yes. But did I *go*?

No.

I panicked. Straight-up, cold-sweat, short-of-breath *panicked*. I blurted out "No" like a complete idiot, and the look on her face gutted me. The shock. The hurt. The immediate shutdown.

I hated myself in that moment. Because I'd made her feel unwanted. Rejected. Again. Like the *one* guy she trusted to be safe and fun had suddenly yanked the rug out from under her.

And yeah, I wanted her. I still wanted her. But sleeping with Ellie would've blown the whole thing up. It would've been a turning point we couldn't come back from.

Because I was still me. Still the guy who can't make it past the three-month mark with a woman. Still the guy who bails before things get real. Still the guy who, deep down, believes he's wired wrong when it comes to love.

Ellie's been through enough. Her ex was a cheat and a liar. If I'd gone to bed with her last night and then walked away in two weeks—like I always do—I'd be no better than him. Another guy who made her feel like she wasn't enough. And Ellie deserves *so* much more than that.

I should've stopped this sooner. The kissing. The flirting. The way I let her worm her way under my skin. I never should've let it get this far. Hell, I never should've asked her to be my nurse in the first place.

But now? I had to fix it. At least try.

Step one: apologize. Profusely. Maybe she'd forgive me. Probably not.

Step two: call the insurance company and request a new nurse. Someone random. Someone I could keep at arm's length.

And if that new nurse turned out to be a fame-hungry asshole who leaked pictures of me to the tabloids? Fine. Karma. I'd take it.

Because Ellie? I wasn't good enough for her. I'd never be good enough for her.

She needed to go back to her life in Milwaukee. And I needed to let her.

No more kissing. No more hoping. No more pretending I'm anything other than exactly what she's always thought I was.

A mistake.

CHAPTER 38

Later Tuesday morning — Ellie

I walked into Luke's bathroom with my head high and my spine straight, aiming for the perfect vibe: "utter professional" with a side of "totally unfazed."

Last night hadn't been a big deal. It couldn't be. We'd agreed on kissing. I'd tried to take things further. He'd hit the brakes. End of story.

Fine, my pride had taken a hit. But I wasn't going to let him see that. I was a grown woman. I could handle a little rejection. We were going back to being friends. Just friends.

No. Big. Deal.

We didn't speak while I changed the dressing on his shoulder. He winced a little when I ripped off the tape, but that was purely because I was in a hurry—not at all because I was quietly fuming. Definitely not. I had a call with Mary from the hospital in fifteen minutes, and I was trying to be efficient.

"Look, Ellie, I'm sorr—"

"Nope." I shook my head and reached for the cotton balls. *Maybe* I dabbed a bit harder than necessary. "Not necessary."

"What do you mean 'nope'?" he asked, brows drawing together.

"You're not going to apologize." I grabbed fresh gauze and tape.

"I didn't mean to—"

"Luke," I said with a smile that could cut glass. "Really. No apology needed. You were right to stop things. Thank you." Okay, maybe the "thank you" was dipped in sarcasm, but I still said it.

"I still feel like a jerk."

I didn't disagree.

"Look," I said, securing the gauze with brisk efficiency. "Let's just admit it—we never should've started kissing in the first place. It was a bad idea. There was tequila. It doesn't mean we can't be friends."

He looked visibly relieved, which—frankly—made me want to throw the tape roll at his head.

"So…we're good?" he asked, giving me that hopeful, boyish look.

"We're fine," I said, giving his (perfect, infuriating) shoulder a pat. "Now, I've got a call. I'll head back to my room."

I turned to go, ready to leave with my dignity intact.

"Wait—Ellie. There's something else I wanted to tell you."

I paused, bracing myself for more apologizing, more "I respect you too much" nonsense. I turned slowly, arms crossed. "What's that?"

He pulled his shirt on, not quite meeting my gaze. "I talked to the insurance company this morning. They're sending a new nurse."

My stomach dropped. "Excuse me?"

"I called them right after I got up," he said, too casual. "You've done more than enough. You should be back in Milwaukee, working on your charity event, not stuck here babysitting me. So the plane's gassed up and ready. The pilot will be there at six."

Wait—what?

"You're sending me home?"

"I'm fixing things," he said with that same maddening, earnest smile. "This isn't fair to you. I pulled you into this. You shouldn't have to deal with—"

"You're firing me," I cut in flatly. "After all this, you're firing me."

His hand landed gently on my shoulder, and he said, "I just want to do the right thing. And the donation—of course —it still stands."

The. *Donation*? Oh, he *was* serious.

I stared at him, pulse pounding, teeth clenched so tight I was one patronizing word away from an actual explosion. But no. No, I wasn't doing that. Not anymore. Post-therapy Ellie had better tools than public meltdowns.

"Great," I said with a perfectly polite smile. "I'll go pack."

Then I turned on my heel and walked out.

By the time I reached the bedroom door, a string of silent curse words were flying through my head on repeat. And still —still—that awful, painful lump was stuck in my throat.

This is what you wanted, I told myself. Normalcy. Boundaries. Clean break. This was the smart thing.

So why did it feel like my chest had cracked open?

CHAPTER 39

I didn't know where I was going until I was knocking on Meg's door.

When it opened, she was barefoot in leggings and a hoodie that read *Jane Austen is My Home Girl*. Her hair was in a high ponytail, eyeliner smudged like she'd been…

I glanced past her to see Jeremy was lying on the bed.

Oh, damn. "I'm sorry," I began.

"You okay?" she asked immediately, grabbing my hand and squeezing it. "You look pale."

I shook my head.

Without another word, she pulled me inside.

Jeremy took one look at my face and stood up. "I'll give you two some space."

He kissed Meg's forehead, gave me a warm smile that only made me feel worse, and disappeared out the door.

The second it shut behind him, I sank onto the edge of the bed like I couldn't stand on my own anymore.

Meg sat beside me, legs folded up, voice low. "What happened?"

"I'm leaving," I said.

Her face fell. "Ellie…"

"It's not what you think. He asked me to go."

"What?"

"He's already hired a new nurse."

"Are you kidding me?" She was already up again and headed for the door.

"Wait," I said.

She stopped.

I took a long, deep breath. "I *want* to go."

She turned back to face me and frowned. "Why?"

I shook my head. My eyes filled with tears. "I can't do this, Meg. I can't stay here pretending I'm not falling for him."

Meg let out a long sigh. Then she padded over and put a hand on my shoulder. "You're not pretending very well," she said with a wry smile.

"I know."

Meg sat beside me, pulling the blanket around both our legs like we were eighteen again, sneaking wine coolers in her bedroom and whispering about boys.

"When I asked him to spend the night with me, and he said no, it felt… Like just rejection…all over again."

"He's scared," Meg said immediately.

I blew out another breath. "I am too."

Meg was quiet for a beat. "Ellie, maybe he was trying to respect what you asked for. You know? Casual. No strings."

"Or maybe he just doesn't want to fight for someone like me."

She frowned. "Someone like you?"

I rubbed my hands over my face. "I'm not glamorous. I'm

not a fan girl. I'm a nurse who wears comfortable shoes to work and falls for men who don't stay."

Meg turned to face me. "Ellie, he's not your ex. And you're not the girl you were after him."

I sighed. "I don't know who I am when I'm not trying to hold everything together."

"That's because you've been surviving for so long, you forgot what it feels like to just *want* something."

I swallowed, then nodded. "I wanted this to be different."

"Then don't leave." She squeezed my fingers.

"I can't stay. I can't be just another woman who got tangled up in his spotlight."

Meg put her hand on my shoulder. "You're not tangled, Ellie. You're the steady thing he never saw coming."

"I don't want to be the one he almost loved," I whispered.

"Then maybe you have to let him figure out whether he's ready to love you fully." Meg's voice was soft.

My throat tightened.

"Don't leave tonight," Meg said. "I think he just needs time."

I shook my head. "I can't do another goodbye. And I need space."

Meg nodded slowly. "Okay. Then promise me something."

"What?"

"That this isn't the last chapter. That you'll let him find you."

I didn't answer. Because I didn't know.

CHAPTER 40

Tuesday night — Luke

I stood at the window of Ellie's guest room, watching the Range Rover pull away from the garage. Headed for the airport. Headed back to Milwaukee.

Back to her life.

Exactly as it should be.

But as soon as the gates closed behind the car, I realized I'd been holding my breath. I let it out slowly, like letting go of something I wasn't ready to lose.

The room was still. Too still.

I turned from the window and walked to the bed. Her bed. I picked up the pillow she'd slept on and brought it to my face. It still smelled like her—warm vanilla. God, that scent. I wanted to lock it in my memory forever.

I exhaled and dropped the pillow back onto the bed.

Would it be weird to tell the house cleaners not to touch this room? Yeah. Definitely. Miss Havisham-level weird.

I walked out of the room and into the hallway. Everything felt…hollow. Too clean. Too quiet. I descended the stairs and stepped into the kitchen, where the refrigerator hummed softly, the only sound in the house.

Linda had left dinner like I'd asked. One plate. Just one.

Before, that wouldn't have meant anything. But now? Now it stared back at me like a neon sign flashing *alone*.

Meg and Jeremy had plans again tonight.

I opened the fridge, grabbed the plate, microwaved it, and sat down at the counter. I stared at the creamed spinach and tilapia like it was an accusation.

Dolly wasn't even in the room with me. She was still in the mudroom, parked at the door Ellie had walked out of, like she half-expected her to come back.

Hell, so did I.

I ran a hand over my face and let my fork idle on the edge of the plate. What did any of this matter? The mansion. The Miami condo. The lake house in Green Bay. Every square inch of it was quiet. Empty. Useless.

Because she was gone.

And it wasn't just that she was gone—it was how I'd let her go. How I'd pushed her away with some twisted idea of protecting her from me.

I'd hurt women before. I'd messed up relationships. Disappointed. Walked away.

But this?

This was the first time I knew I'd regret it for the rest of my life.

CHAPTER 41

Friday — Luke

It had been three days. I should've been able to write something.

That was always the plan. Write it out. Bleed it into chords. Turn pain into something that sounded less like failure and more like closure.

But the studio was useless tonight. Worse than useless. It felt *wrong*.

I sat in the dark, the only light coming from the desk lamp in the corner and the blue hue of the laptop screen—still open to the blank lyrics file I hadn't added a word to in two hours.

The guitar was propped beside me, untouched.

My left arm still ached, but that wasn't the problem.

The problem was Ellie was gone.

And I had made sure of it.

I'd done the *rational* thing. The responsible thing. I'd told her I'd hired a new nurse. Gave her a clean off-ramp. Said it like it was good news. Said it like I wasn't handing her a ticket out of my life and daring her to take it.

And she did.

I hadn't even tried to stop her.

The song still refused to come. I picked up the guitar anyway, letting it settle against me like muscle memory would save me. I strummed once. Dull. Off-key. My fingers didn't follow through.

I dropped it back onto its stand and shoved my hand into my hair.

What the hell was I doing?

I couldn't write. Couldn't sleep. Couldn't eat. Dolly hadn't left the front door. She kept perking up at every sound like it might be Eliie.

Like she might walk back through the door if we just sat still long enough.

At four p.m., I caved.

Texted Dr. Heinselberg. Begged for a last-minute session.

By seven, I was in my room with my laptop open, the webcam staring me down like it knew I didn't have answers.

Dr. H appeared on screen, framed by a bookshelf, sipping from her favorite mug—the one that said *I paused my Netflix binge for this.* It always made me feel both judged and weirdly comforted.

She set the mug down and folded her hands. "So."

That's all she said.

Just *so.*

I dragged a hand down my face. "She left."

Her brows lifted gently. "Ellie?"

"Yeah."

"The nurse?"

"Yeah."

"The nurse I've highly suspected for the last week that you have feelings for?"

I gave a humorless laugh. "You were right."

She nodded once. "How did that feel?"

"Like someone took a hammer to my chest. Which, for the record, is not the injured side."

"Why did she leave?"

"Because I told her I hired a new nurse."

Dr. H tilted her head. "And how exactly did you phrase that?"

"I said that I appreciated everything she did. That she could go home now."

"And she just…did?"

I exhaled. "Yeah. She left."

Her silence stretched just long enough to be uncomfortable.

"I thought I was doing the right thing," I said. "Letting her off the hook."

"Was she on a hook?"

"No," I muttered. "She was…amazing. Kind. Funny. Smart. And yeah, okay, maybe a little intense about my shoulder exercises, but—God. She was *here*, you know? She showed up."

"Did you tell her any of that?"

"No."

Dr. H sat back. "Luke. What do you want?"

"What do I want or what am I going to do?" I snapped. "Because those are different things."

Her voice stayed calm. "What do you *want*?"

I didn't hesitate.

"I want to chase her," I said. "I want to go to Milwaukee and tell her that I want to try. That I'm all in."

She nodded. "And what are you afraid of?"

The answer came too fast. "That I'm not enough. That she'll look at me and see the guy who spent years avoiding anything real. The guy who slept around, ducked out on real conversations, and made everything a joke."

"Is that who you are now?"

"I don't know," I said honestly. "I think I'm changing. I've got boundaries. I have a rescue dog. A full-time chef. A laundry schedule. A therapist."

Her lips quirked. "All the marks of emotional maturity."

I cracked a smile for the first time in days. It didn't last.

"I didn't know I could feel like this," I said quietly. "Like her not being here actually hurts. Physically."

"That's love," she said simply.

I cracked a smile. "Feels a lot like panic."

"It's supposed to. Love doesn't cancel out fear. It just gives you something *worth* being afraid for."

I stared at the screen.

She leaned in. "Go to her. But not to fix it. Not to win. Go to tell the truth. To stand in it."

I nodded slowly, the words catching on something raw in my chest.

"I think she might be my person," I said.

Dr. H smiled gently. "Then tell her that. And if she walks away, you'll survive. But you'll know you *showed up*. For her. And for yourself."

I sat with that. And I'd never been more afraid.

CHAPTER 42

Friday — Milwaukee — Ellie

I hadn't unpacked.

The suitcase sat by the door like a question mark I was still too emotionally hungover to answer. I'd been home for seventy-two hours and already everything about this place felt smaller. Duller. Like the color had faded just slightly, as if Nashville had existed in higher resolution.

I stood at the kitchen counter, nursing lukewarm coffee and trying not to obsessively check my phone. I hadn't heard from him. No texts. No calls.

Except one.

Last night, just after midnight, my phone lit up with *Luke Knightley*, and my heart had exploded like a startled flock of birds.

I hadn't answered.

Not on purpose—I was convinced I would throw up. And anyway, I wanted him to think I was too busy to talk. He hadn't left a voicemail. Just…silence.

I hadn't called back either.

I told myself it was better that way.

He didn't leave a message because he didn't know what to say. Because he'd already said everything by hiring a new nurse and letting me walk out of his life without blinking.

Still, I couldn't help opening Instagram like some kind of masochist. Just to see.

Just to check.

And there it was.

A photo.

A blurry but unmistakable image from some Nashville tabloid account: *Luke Knightley spotted at dinner with mystery brunette. Sources say she's "a longtime friend and stylist" but the body language says otherwise* ✶ ✶ .

She was laughing. Leaning close. One hand on his uninjured arm.

My stomach dropped.

Did he feel safe with her? Did he try to kiss her?

It didn't matter that I knew what it *could* be. That it could be innocent. That it could be a business meeting or an old friend or just another snapshot of his life that I didn't belong in anymore.

All I saw was confirmation.

Confirmation that I was right to leave.

That I had been one of many.

That I had gotten too close and then been replaced with a single phone call and a press-friendly smile.

My phone rang and I nearly jumped. Oh, thank God. It was Gran.

"Hello?"

"You still moping over that boy?"

"I'm not—"

"Don't lie to me, Ellie-bean. I've known you since before you had eyebrows. You sat at my table last night, pushed peas around your plate like you were shooting pool, and gave me the sketchiest of sketchy details. 'It didn't work out, Gran.' That's all I got. Like you were recapping a parking ticket."

I sighed, sinking into one of the kitchen chairs. "It's complicated."

"It always is with men who look like Greek gods and kiss like they've got something to prove. Doesn't mean you should let 'em turn you into a zombie."

"I'm fine."

"Honey, you've been wearing the same sad ponytail for three days. That boy did a number on you."

I let out a weak laugh. "How did you know about my ponytail?"

"So you admit he did a number on you?"

"No. I just… I thought maybe it meant something." I let out a deep sigh.

"It did," she said, her voice gentler now. "Even if it's over, that doesn't mean it didn't matter. But let me tell you something, and listen close because I'm not repeating myself: when a man lets you walk away without chasing you, that's not romance, it's a gift receipt. You don't beg to keep something that doesn't fit."

I blinked. "That was actually kind of profound."

"I have my moments," she sniffed. "Now put on some real pants, go outside, and for the love of God, stop stalking his Instagram like a sad teenager in a Netflix original. He's not the only man in the world with good hair and dimples."

I smiled for the first time that morning. "Thanks, Gran."

"Anytime. Now go. And don't forget—clean underwear. You never know who you'll run into."

Gran hung up.

I stared at the phone for a second, heart a little lighter, coffee tasting a little less like disappointment.

Gran was right, of course.

As usual.

Same time – Luke

I STARED AT MY PHONE, thumb hovering over Ellie's contact.

I'd already drafted the message three times. Deleted it. Redrafted it. Considered calling. Considered flying there. Considered never speaking again just to spare us both the heartbreak of another *almost*.

I'd already called her an hour ago.

The line rang twice.

Then stopped.

No answer.

I didn't leave a voicemail. What was I supposed to say?

Hi, sorry I pushed you away with emotional whiplash, then hired your replacement like it was nothing. Also, I think I might love you. Hope the weather in Milwaukee's nice.

I stared at the screen.

Coward.

Dolly looked up from the doorway, head tilted, ears perked like she could sense that something important had just not happened.

I scratched behind her ear. My phone buzzed.

Oh, Jesus. A text from dad.

> Hey Sport, saw you online today. Hot-looking date. Good for you. Hey, if you ever have a gig in Vegas, look me up. Would love to see you. And Meg.

And there it was. My reason for knowing that I'd never be a good husband. My father. A man who still called me "sport" like I was thirteen. A man who hadn't made my mother happy a day in their marriage.

Everyone always said I looked like him, took after him.

Well, not this time. Ellie didn't deserve the shit my mom had to go through. If I needed a sign to keep me from reaching out, there it was in text form.

But what was that about a hot-looking date?

I searched the most famous celebrity gossip site. The one that had all the supposed "late-breaking" news. Half of which wasn't true.

And there it was. A picture from dinner last night—a meeting with my stylist, Lauren. The paparazzi had snapped us outside a restaurant and twisted it into something it wasn't.

I stared at the caption.

Mystery brunette.

Damn it.

Ellie would see that. She'd see it and think the worst.

And I couldn't even blame her.

CHAPTER 43

Monday — Ellie

I hadn't expected to get emotional walking back through the doors of the children's hospital, but the second I stepped into the fourth-floor hallway, something tight and warm curled in my chest.

The familiar hum of monitors. The scent of disinfectant and crayons. The muffled laughter from the playroom. It all felt like home and memory and a hundred reasons to keep going.

I stopped at the nurse's station to sign in and was immediately ambushed by Mindy.

"You're back!" she shouted, barreling toward me in fuzzy avocado socks and a unicorn hoodie. "I saw on the calendar that you were coming in, and I told everyone to be cool. And then I absolutely did not act cool."

I laughed, catching her in a hug. She felt smaller somehow, but lighter too.

"You look amazing," I said, pulling back. "Are those new earrings?"

She beamed. "They're tiny bagels. Etsy."

"You continue to be my style icon."

She grinned, then leaned in conspiratorially. "Now, please tell me you and Luke Knightley are in love and getting married soon."

I raised a brow. "Not quite."

"But you *are* dating?"

"You seriously need to stop reading Wattpad."

"That's no fun."

"Believe me. If anything interesting happens in my love life that you need to know, I'll be sure to keep you posted."

Her face fell, but her smile quickly returned when I pulled the small bag of sugar-free chocolates out of my tote.

"Oh, thank you. These are my favorite," she said.

I left her feeling lighter, but also heavier in the best way—weighted by belonging. By purpose.

At the end of the hall, I found Dr. Waters bent over a chart at the nurses' station. Her eyes flicked up when she saw me.

"Well, well. Look what the cat dragged back."

I grinned. "Hi, Lena."

"You look different," she said, straightening. "Less frayed. Less caffeine-fueled panic in the eyes."

"I took your advice."

"About the spa or the break?"

"Both, technically."

She tilted her head. "You stayed gone longer than I thought you would."

"I needed it."

"Did it help?"

I paused, thinking of Luke's voice in my ear, his laugh, the way he kissed like he was memorizing something. "Yeah. It did."

Dr. Waters eyed me for a long moment, then smiled.

"Good. Because if you try to work a double this week, I'll have security drag you out."

"Noted."

She turned back to the chart, but not before muttering, "Took you long enough."

I started down the hall, letting the familiar beeps and voices settle around me. I didn't know exactly what came next. But I knew I could hold both: the parts of me that healed others, and the part that was still learning to heal myself.

CHAPTER 44

A Thursday in August — Ellie

I turned in a slow circle at the center of the grand ballroom, taking it all in. Crystal chandeliers sparkled above white-linen tables blooming with white roses and glowing jasmine candles. Music would fill the air on Saturday night. There would be dancing, bidding wars, raffle prizes, and smiling donors swilling champagne. The Sixteenth Annual Milwaukee Children's Hospital Gala was officially going to be magical.

And it had worked.

The venue had been donated by a generous hotel conglomerate, and dozens of local businesses had chipped in to transform the space into something out of a fairy tale. But as I surveyed the scene, I had to admit—this fairy tale had a few Nashville fingerprints on it. The white roses, the jasmine candles…they reminded me a little too much of Luke's house. Of Luke.

Okay, fine. I may have taken more than a little inspiration from his decorator. But I was five hundred miles away, and what she didn't know wouldn't hurt her.

When I got back to Milwaukee two months ago, I buried myself in gala planning like my sanity depended on it. Which, if I was being honest, it kind of did. I already had a guaranteed $250,000 donation (thanks, Luke), but I was still determined to make this year's fundraiser the best one yet. Whenever my mind tried to drift to Nashville—specifically to a certain blue-eyed musician—I yanked it right back to seating charts and silent auction spreadsheets.

And it worked. Mostly.

There were slip-ups, sure. Moments when I remembered the weight of Luke's hand at the small of my back or the way his voice dipped into a growl when he whispered my name. And yeah, okay, sometimes the memory of him kissing down my neck still made me squeeze my thighs together. But that was just biology. Luke Knightley was objectively hot and, as it turned out, criminally good at making out.

It wasn't just the physical stuff though. Sometimes I found myself thinking about the unexpected parts of him— the guy who read Tolstoy, named his dog Dolly, and had never actually had a one-night stand. The guy who paid for a built-in dog bed for his dog's best friend. Who looked so boyish when he asked me to go to Miami with him, like he genuinely didn't believe I'd say yes.

But the hardest part hadn't been the memories. It had been the call.

A few weeks back, a gossip site ran a blurry photo of the two of us entering the restaurant through a side door in Miami. *Luke Knightley's Mystery Date?* the headline read. Wow. That was some really old news. I laughed when my friend Morgan sent it to me. But that night, when my phone lit up with Luke's name, I nearly passed out.

I answered. Tried to play it cool. Said something dumb

like, "Oh, that?" Like I'd forgotten the image of his hand on my hip burned into my skin.

We kept it light. Polite. He asked about the gala. I asked about his shoulder. We exchanged two vague "great"s and hung up. I stared at my phone for hours after, waiting for a second call that never came.

And then, the next morning, I got up and dove headfirst back into linen napkin swatches and donor lists.

Now, as I stood in the glowing ballroom, I was proud of what I'd built. I'd done something good. Something lasting. And I had no intention of letting my short-lived detour with a rock star cloud that.

In fact, I had a date next week.

Morgan had been trying to set me up with Dr. Sam-from-Pediatrics for nearly a year, and I'd finally relented. He was divorced, no kids, kind, stable—her words. The opposite of Luke Knightley in every possible way.

And that was the point.

After my minor meltdown in Tennessee, I realized I'd been hiding from dating. Avoiding anything that might hurt. So when Luke showed up, confident and chaotic and charming as hell, I'd mistaken chemistry for something deeper. That was on me.

But Sam? Sam could be fun. A step back into the real world. And if the night ended with a kiss—or more—I wouldn't hate it.

This wasn't a big deal.

None of it was a big deal.

I was moving forward. Starting fresh. And I was going to enjoy it.

CHAPTER 45

Friday – Luke

The second Meg walked into the studio, I knew I was screwed. Arms crossed. Jaw set. That classic sister-glare locked and loaded. I didn't need her to speak to know she was about to hand me my ass.

I kept strumming my guitar anyway, pretending to be oblivious. Not that it would help.

My shoulder and arm may have healed, but my heart? Jury was still out.

Meg didn't say a word at first—just stood there with her glasses perched on her nose and one impatient foot tapping like a ticking bomb.

Dr. H underestimated me. Or I overestimated myself. Ever since our talk that night about Ellie leaving, I've pretended as if it never happened. Told myself again and again that I was doing the noble thing, the right thing, the best thing for Ellie.

And did I feel like complete shit? Yes. But that was my problem. Ellie deserved better than what I had to give.

Meg, meanwhile, had been strangely silent on the subject for weeks. I'd started to believe maybe she wasn't going to say anything. That I was off the hook.

Until I saw her face just now.

"Well?" Meg finally snapped.

"Well what?" I asked, not looking up.

"Jeremy and I are flying to Milwaukee. Tomorrow is the charity gala. Ring any bells?"

I stilled my fingers on the strings. Just hearing the words *charity gala* made my chest tighten. "Tell Ellie I said hi."

Meg's nostrils flared. "That's it? You want me to pass along *hi* like she's just an old classmate and not the woman you made out with for a week straight?"

I set the guitar upright against my thigh and met her eyes. "What do you want me to say, Meg?"

She rolled her eyes. "Oh, I don't know. Maybe something other than the dumbest line in the history of dumb lines. You let her leave, Luke."

"She *chose* to leave."

"You gave her a plane and practically shoved her into it."

"She wanted to go."

"You don't know that." Meg's voice cracked, and her foot stopped tapping. "You could have *asked* her. But you didn't. And you haven't done a damn thing about it since."

I looked away. "You weren't there. You don't know the full story."

"Well, here's what I *do* know," she said. "I know *you*. And I know when you're hurting. You've been down here writing songs and hiding for weeks. You miss her."

"So what if I do?" I snapped. "It doesn't change the facts. I'm not cut out for relationships. We both know that."

"You're not *Dad*, Luke."

Oof. That landed hard. My throat went tight. I clenched my jaw.

"You're nothing like him," she continued.

I exhaled slowly and leaned forward, pressing my hand to my forehead. "Remember the way Mom used to look at him, Meg? Like she couldn't believe she'd ever trusted him. Like she hated herself for it. If I ever saw that look on someone I care about—on *Ellie*—I'd lose it."

Meg walked over and placed a gentle hand on my shoulder. "You won't. You've always protected the people you care about. You protect me. You took care of Mom when Dad couldn't. You're not some self-absorbed jerk who bails when things get hard. You're loyal and smart and brave enough to chase your dreams."

I said nothing, still staring down.

"You got into Stanford. You left a cushy job. You built this band from nothing. You bet on yourself over and over. And now you're too scared to bet on someone who made you happier than I've seen you in years?"

Her words sliced through me.

"Ellie's not some girl you hook up with and forget," she added. "She's the real thing. Wife material."

"I *know*," I said, barely a whisper.

Meg's eyes softened. "Then don't be a coward now. Fight for her."

She turned to go, then glanced back. "Oh. One more thing."

I braced myself.

"She has a date next week. Cute. Single. *Doctor*. You've got about five minutes before someone else realizes what a catch she is."

And then she left, flats clicking on the hardwood floor, while I sat there, heart pounding, pretending my sister hadn't just thrown a full-force grenade straight at my heart.

CHAPTER 46

Later Friday night — Luke

After Meg—agent of emotional chaos that she was—left the studio, I couldn't focus on a damn thing. Couldn't write. Couldn't play. Could barely breathe. She'd dropped that little bomb—*Ellie has a date next week with a doctor*—like it was no big deal.

But it *was* a big deal.

And Meg knew it. That's exactly why she said it.

Yeah, I'd been off since Ellie left. I'd told myself it was just recovery. Rehab. Work. Therapy. I'd been through hell, and who wouldn't be a little wrecked after the year I'd had? But deep down, I knew the truth. I hadn't felt like myself since the night I let her walk out of this house.

Scratch that—I hadn't felt like *me* until she walked *into* this house.

I'd told myself I was protecting her. That I wasn't relationship material. That I was just like my dad. But the truth? The truth was, with Ellie, I hadn't *wanted* to be that guy. I'd wanted to be *better*. For her. With her.

In the two months since she'd left, I'd gotten better. Really better. I'd kept up therapy. Gone out in public again. Talked to fans. Signed autographs. Took pictures. Posed with people. And the entire time, I knew exactly why I could do it.

Because of her.

Ellie made me feel safe. Like home. Like *me*, but more—me *at my best*.

And yeah, I'd gone over every relationship I'd ever had, every woman I'd dated since I was sixteen, trying to figure out why it had never worked. The answer was obvious now: none of them were Ellie. She'd always been the girl in the background—loyal, funny, sharp as hell. She didn't just challenge me. She saw me. And she didn't run.

Meg was right. Ellie was the one I should have fought for.

Dr. H hadn't brought it up again. I expected that was one of her Jedi mind tricks. But she had said something that looped through my head on constant repeat.

"Sometimes other people don't just hurt us by what they did. They control us by what we let their damage keep us from doing."

Damn. That hit.

Add Meg's voice to the chorus—*You're not Dad*—and suddenly all my excuses felt hollow. I'd been so afraid of becoming him that I was letting that fear make my decisions for me. And Ellie was the collateral damage.

No more.

The truth had been there all along. In every kiss. Every laugh. Every time I reached for Ellie without thinking.

She wasn't just someone I liked. She was *it*. She always had been.

And now she was going on a date with some doctor? *Hell. No.*

I stood up, shoved the guitar back in its case, and headed for the door. If I had to call a dozen people to make this happen, I would. If I had to show up uninvited, I would. And if I had to make an ass of myself in front of half of Milwaukee, I'd do that too.

I'd played the odds before. This time, I was all in.

And I wasn't leaving without Ellie Hoffman.

CHAPTER 47

Saturday night — Milwaukee — The Children's Hospital Charity Gala — Ellie

I'd been running around all evening trying to make everything perfect. Mary kept telling me to relax and enjoy myself, but relaxation wasn't exactly my spiritual gift. Apparently, the metaphorical stick was back where it lived—firmly lodged.

I'd triple-checked the silent auction bids, interrogated the caterers until they politely kicked me out of the kitchen, and rotated the crystal rose vases until one of the volunteers asked if I was okay.

Meg appeared beside me with a glass of champagne and a knowing smile.

"You did it, Ellie," she said, handing me the flute. "This place looks like a fairy tale."

"Thanks." I beamed, pride bubbling just under the surface.

Still, the pride came with an edge of nerves. This night was the culmination of months of planning—sleepless nights, dozens of Zoom calls, and an endless back-and-forth with the hospital board. It wasn't just an event. It was proof that I could make something good. Something lasting. For kids like Mindy. For people who needed more than hope—they needed action. And maybe, for once, I needed it too. I needed to believe I was more than a nurse in scrubs with a fix-it streak and a tendency to run from my own feelings.

"And you," Meg added, giving me a once-over, "look like the fairy godmother of said fairy tale. A hot one."

I grinned. My strapless pink satin gown had taken too many shopping trips to find, but tonight, I finally felt like it was worth it. Grace Kelly-meets-modern-gala chic. Meg, in her sparkly black peplum dress and glittery flats—because she claimed to have Hobbit feet that wouldn't fit in heels—looked like a firecracker herself.

"Where's Jeremy?" I asked, glancing around the ballroom.

"Poor guy got cornered by some dude asking about woodworking. I thought it would be fun small talk until he asked if he makes cutting boards." She winced. "Apparently, that's the woodworker version of asking a nurse if they just hand out Band-Aids."

I laughed. "Noted. No cutting board jokes at future wedding receptions."

Meg waggled her brows. "Speaking of weddings…still going out with Dr. Hottie next week?"

I lifted my chin. "Yes. But it's just a date. Don't you dare start picking out our future children's names."

She sipped her champagne. "Fine. But color me curious."

We both turned as the lights dimmed slightly. I checked my watch. "The band's up next," I said, nodding toward the curtained stage. "They've been tucked behind there for hours. Apparently they're too 'in the zone' to be disturbed. Mary banned me from going back there. Seem like snobs."

Meg's eyes sparkled as she raised her glass. "Well, here's to delicate artists."

"They're good though. I saw them a couple of times this summer. Great stage presence. Nothing too heavy—just a fun, crowd-friendly sound. They're called Lazy Sunday."

Meg choked slightly on her drink.

"What?" I asked.

She just grinned. "Nothing. Cheers to Lazy Sunday."

As we toasted, Mary suddenly strode onto the stage and adjusted the microphone.

I frowned. "Wait. Why is *she* up there? I'm supposed to introduce the band."

Meg caught my arm before I could storm toward the stage. "Just watch," she whispered, barely containing her grin.

Mary smiled out at the crowd. "Good evening, and welcome to the Sixteenth Annual Milwaukee Children's Hospital Charity Gala!"

Applause filled the ballroom. I glared at Meg. She nodded calmly toward the stage.

"Before we begin the silent auction," Mary continued, "we have a very special surprise. This band has not only agreed to perform for free tonight, they're also donating $250,000— and matching every dollar donated during the gala."

The room erupted into cheers. And then she said it.

"Please welcome Milwaukee's own…Whiskey Smoke!"

The curtains swung open.

And there he was.

Luke. With his guitar slung across his chest, standing center stage in jeans, boots, a sapphire shirt, and a brown leather jacket. No sling. No hesitation.

Just him. Here.

The first notes of their biggest hit rang out, and the crowd lost it. People clapped, swayed, danced. But I just… froze.

Meg leaned over, voice gleeful. "You okay?"

"You *knew*," I whispered, my mouth still open.

"Maybe. Recently." She sipped her drink, smug as ever. "Oh, and FYI—he's not here for the gala."

I stared at her, stunned. "What are you talking about?"

"He's here for *you*, Ellie."

I whipped my head back toward the stage just as the song ended and Luke stepped up to the mic.

"Hi, everyone. I'm Luke Knightley. I was born and raised right here in Milwaukee."

The room cheered again.

"I want to dedicate this next song to someone I've known most of my life. Someone who's always been there for my sister—and who was there for me when I needed her most. She also happens to be the reason we're all here tonight: *Ms. Ellie Hoffman*."

I blinked hard, and I didn't miss the emphasis he placed on my honorific.

Meg bumped my shoulder. "Still think he's not here for you?"

On stage, Luke continued. "Ellie's the kind of person who makes you better just by being around her. And I'm here tonight not just to play, but to ask her to give me a real chance. I want to take her on a date. I want to be her boyfriend. And if she says yes, I'd be the luckiest guy in this whole damn city."

A collective *aww* rose from the crowd.

I pressed a hand to my mouth, tears threatening. "Oh my God," I breathed. "Is this really happening?"

"Looks like it," Meg said, beaming.

Luke stepped back, strummed the opening notes of a ballad, and sang.

I remember a girl
With sunshine in her hair
Smile in her eyes
But too much to bear...

My knees nearly gave out. He was singing *Summer Nights.* For me. *About* me?

The minute the song ended, he took a deep breath. "And here's a new one. I just wrote it recently. It's not on any album yet. Y'all will be the first to hear it."

Another cheer from the crowd.

I couldn't move. I couldn't breathe.

Luke scanned the crowd, paused, and found me. His breath hitched—barely—but I saw it.

I felt it.

Everyone else disappeared.

"This one's for someone who made it impossible to keep pretending," he said softly.

He didn't look away.

Neither did I.

And then he started to play.

I didn't hear the lyrics. Not really. Not all the way through.

There was a line about a girl who stopped the world with a whisper and hands that knew how to heal things no one could see. A line about mistakes. A line about leaving. And then:

If you ask, I'll try.
If you stay, I'll stay.
If you want me—I'm yours.
All the way.

My hands were shaking.

Meg whispered something—probably "Are you okay?" or "Oh my God" or "He wrote that for you"—but I couldn't answer. Couldn't even nod.

When the song ended, Luke handed off his guitar, leapt from the stage, and wove through the crowd until he found me.

"Ellie."

My name on his lips undid me. I was shaking my head, like none of this could be real.

"That song… That's about me?" I could barely speak.

He nodded. "Both of them." He bit his lip, looking almost shy.

"Oh, my God," I whispered, staring at the floor in a daze.

He ducked his head to catch my eye. "Come with me?" He looked hopeful, anxious.

When I nodded, his shoulders relaxed. He grabbed my hand and led me away, through doors and down some hallways until we were behind the stage.

We stood alone under the soft glow of a sconce. The ballroom noise was muted by distance and too many unsaid things.

I folded my arms and searched his face. "Why now?"

His jaw flexed. "Because I finally stopped letting fear win."

I didn't speak.

"I let you leave," he said, stepping closer. "I thought it was what you needed. I thought protecting you meant pushing you away."

"And now?" I asked, voice barely above a whisper.

"Now I know that I was wrong. That I was scared. That I didn't know how to be loved by someone who *saw me.*"

I looked up at him.

He looked wrecked. But still hopeful. Open in a way that made me want to cry and shake him all at once.

"You know I'm not perfect," he continued. "I'm still learning how to show up. But I want to try. I want to build something with you, Ellie. No stage. No spotlight. Just us."

Tears burned the back of my throat. Before I could speak again, he wrapped his arms around me, lifted me, and spun me in a full circle.

"I'm sorry I let you go," he said, voice low. "I love you. I think I've always loved you. I can't promise you I'll never make a mistake, but I will *never* hurt you. I'll never leave. Just…give me a shot?"

My heart flipped. "Are you serious?"

"Oh, yeah," he whispered. Then added with a grin, "And next time you ask me to spend the night with you? The answer's going to be hell yes."

And with that, he kissed me.

And reader, I kissed him right back.

EPILOGUE

The next May — Nashville — Ellie

Moving to Nashville turned out to be the best decision I ever made.

Not that I did it right away. Oh no. I made Luke earn it. He stayed in Milwaukee for a couple of months to properly court me, crashing on Meg's couch like the good old days. I needed to make sure the man had staying power before I uprooted my entire life. Turns out I probably would've moved anyway, because two weeks after the gala, Meg told me that she and Jeremy were planning to relocate to Nashville too—after the school year ended.

Meg was finally making the leap to writing romance novels full time, and Jeremy was moving his woodworking business to Music City, where Luke's wealthy friends would probably keep him elbow-deep in walnut and oak for the foreseeable future.

And that wasn't even the juiciest part.

Apparently, *Mrs. Timms* had never been sick at all. Meg had orchestrated the "emergency return to Milwaukee" because she *knew* that if Luke and I were left alone, we'd end up horizontal in record time. And it had been *Mrs. Timms's* idea to fake an illness. I'm not sure what kind of scam artist Jeremy had living next door, but I couldn't even be mad about it.

Though I did make a mental note: under no circumstances could Mrs. Timms and my Gran ever be introduced. The world would not survive that level of chaos. Modern-day Thelma and Louise didn't need a convertible—they just needed joint custody of a burner phone and a shared vendetta.

And God help us all if they ever got their hands on a bottle of tequila.

Meg admitted she'd played it cool all summer, knowing full well that if she pushed either Luke or me toward each other, we'd both slam on the brakes. She knew us better than we knew ourselves. And now she wore her meddling like a crown. We couldn't fault her. We were together. And happy.

Ridiculously happy.

Luke turned out to be the kind of boyfriend who brought me flowers when he came home and rubbed my feet after long shifts at the hospital. Nashville was warmer and brighter than Milwaukee ever had been. I got a job I loved at Vanderbilt Children's. And yes, I moved into the mansion. (That's not as bougie as it sounds. Okay. Maybe it is.)

Gran was even thinking about relocating, but for now, I made regular visits via Luke's private jet. Which, honestly, still made me giggle every time I boarded it.

Mindy and I still FaceTimed every Friday. She was in remission now—thriving, scarf-free, and sassier than ever. She'd finally received the bone marrow transplant she desperately needed, funded by an anonymous donor I strongly suspected was Luke. He still wouldn't admit it. Typical.

After the gala, Luke and the band went back to the children's wing to perform, and it was livestreamed across social media. We raised another quarter of a million dollars just off donations that night. It had been wild. And wonderful.

Now that Luke's tour was over, he was due home any minute. I'd flown out to see him whenever I could, but long distance hadn't been easy. Still, I never once doubted him. The man called me every night without fail. Meg said he was head over heels. I already knew I was.

And with the tour behind us, there was a new event to concentrate on: Meg and Jeremy's wedding. It was coming up soon.

I found them on the patio, deep in a heated seating chart discussion, with Dolly and Huckie lounging like royalty at their feet.

"What's the drama, lovebirds?"

"Seating chart," Meg said with a huff, tapping her pen.

"Jeremy doesn't understand why Christopher Wentworth can't sit at the table in front of the wedding party," she added.

"Why can't he?" Jeremy asked, genuinely baffled.

"Because your sister, Ariana, will be sitting three feet away," Meg snapped.

"Ooooh," I said, immediately getting it. "Yeah, nope. No good."

"What?" Jeremy looked between us. "Their breakup was, like, ten years ago."

Meg and I gave him matching looks of pity. "Just like a man," I muttered.

Jeremy blinked. "What? It's still a thing?"

"It's *definitely* still a thing," Meg said. "Especially if he shows up with a girlfriend. Ariana's still single."

"She doesn't even talk about it," Jeremy protested.

"Exactly," Meg deadpanned.

Jeremy sighed. "Fine. But I have to invite him—he's one of Luke's best friends."

"Then sit him in the back," Meg said, circling a corner spot. "Like, *way* back. Outer Mongolia, ideally."

I was still laughing when the dogs suddenly leapt to their feet and tore toward the French doors. Luke stepped outside, looking tan, tousled, and totally edible.

"I'm back," he announced.

I launched myself into his arms. He spun me around like he always did now that his arm was healed, and I held on tight, grinning like a loon. Let's just say that what we'd been up to since his shoulder fully recovered made all the kissing from last summer look downright G-rated.

I kissed him senseless, then watched him do the bro-hug-pat thing with Jeremy and give Meg a hug.

"You're just in time to weigh in on the seating chart," I said.

Luke took one look at the papers and held up his hands. "Nope. I'm paying for this wedding. That's the extent of my involvement."

That comment made all three of us laugh. Jeremy and Luke had gone back and forth about who should foot the bill until they settled it the only way two overly competitive men could—poker. Luke had won, obviously. He always did. Meg hadn't protested one bit.

"I can't believe the wedding's barely more than a month away," Meg said, sighing as she stared at the chart.

"Yes, but first..." Jeremy rubbed his hands together. "Vegas, baby."

The joint bachelor/bachelorette party was next weekend. Jeremy's idea, surprisingly. Even Meg, who once needed a spreadsheet and a full-sized day planner to execute a weekend getaway, had said yes without blinking—even though Vegas was also the city where she and Luke's estranged, gambling-addicted father lived.

Luke and I weren't particularly jazzed about the gambling part, but he'd promised me good restaurants, luxury shopping, and maybe even some tequila. Sounded perfect.

I started walking toward the French doors. "Hey, Luke. Come upstairs. I want to show you the suit you're wearing to the wedding. You need to try it on."

"Oh, *I'm sure* that's what you want to show him," Meg said, using air quotes.

"Don't wait dinner on us," I called in a singsong voice, already pulling Luke inside by the hand.

It still hit me sometimes—this life I'd built that felt like it belonged to someone else. The girl who always held everyone else together, who kept the plates spinning no matter what, now had a closet full of scrubs, a key code to a mansion, and a man who looked at her like she was the miracle. Somewhere between the long-distance phone calls and the impromptu visits, between laughter and the late-night confessions, Luke and I had built something solid. Something that felt like it could last.

Because here's the thing: I didn't just move to Nashville.

I let someone in.

I found home.

THANK you for reading Ellie and Luke's story. The next book in the Austen Hunks trilogy is *Marrying Mr. Wentworth*. Find out what happens when Ariana sees Christopher at the bachelor/bachelorette party in Vegas. CLICK HERE TO READ *Marrying Mr. Wentworth* now.

The Debutante Dilemma (Book 3)

The Wallflower Win (Book 4)

Lords in Disguise

The Footman is an Earl (Book 1)

Duke Looks Like a Groomsman (Book 2)

The Marquess Who Loved Me (Book 3)

Save a Horse, Ride a Viscount (Book 4)

Earl Lessons (Book 5)

The Duke is Back (Book 6)

Playful Brides

The Unexpected Duchess (Book 1)

The Accidental Countess (Book 2)

The Unlikely Lady (Book 3)

The Irresistible Rogue (Book 4)

The Unforgettable Hero (Book 4.5)

The Untamed Earl (Book 5)

The Legendary Lord (Book 6)

Never Trust a Pirate (Book 7)

The Right Kind of Rogue (Book 8)

A Duke Like No Other (Book 9)

Kiss Me At Christmas (Book 10)

Mr. Hunt, I Presume (Book 10.5)

No Other Duke But You (Book 11)

Secret Brides

Secrets of a Wedding Night (Book 1)

A Secret Proposal (Book 1.5)

I'd love to keep in touch.

- Visit my website for information about upcoming books, excerpts, and to sign up for my email newsletter: www.ValerieBowmanBooks.com or at www.ValerieBowmanBooks.com/subscribe.
- Join me on Facebook: http://Facebook.com/ValerieBowmanAuthor
- Join me on Instagram: http://www.instagram.com/valeriegbowman/
- Reviews help other readers find books. I appreciate all reviews. Thank you so much for considering it!

Want to read the other Austen Hunks books?

- Hiring Mr. Darcy
- Kissing Mr. Knightley
- Marrying Mr. Wentworth

ABOUT THE AUTHOR

Valerie Bowman grew up in Illinois with six sisters (she's number seven) and a huge supply of romance novels.

After a cold and snowy stint earning a degree in English with a minor in history at Smith College, she moved to Florida the first chance she got.

Valerie now lives in Jacksonville with her family including her two rascally dogs. When she's not writing, she keeps busy reading, traveling, or vacillating between watching crazy reality TV and PBS.

Valerie loves to hear from readers. Find her on the web at www.ValerieBowmanBooks.com.

facebook.com/ValerieBowmanAuthor
instagram.com/valeriegbowman
goodreads.com/Valerie_Bowman
bookbub.com/authors/valerie-bowman
amazon.com/author/valeriebowman